Wooing the Undertaker

LOVE IN APPLE BLOSSOM
BOOK FOUR

KIT MORGAN

Wooing the Undertaker

(Love in Apple Blossom, Book 4)

© 2023 Kit Morgan

Cover design by Angel Creek Press and EDH Designs

❀ Created with Vellum

License Note

This book is licensed for your personal enjoyment only. This book may not be re-sold or given away to other people. If you would like to share this book with another person, please purchase an additional copy for each recipient. If you're reading this book and did not purchase it, or it was not purchased for your use only, then please return and purchase your own copy. Thank you for respecting the hard work of this author.

Chapter One

A *pple Blossom, Montana Territory, on the afternoon of a proposal, 1879*

"You did what?" Wallis Darling said, his voice a mix of shock and disbelief. Had he heard his brother Irving right? Had any of them? Irving had gathered them in the hotel dining room for a big announcement, but this?

Wallis glanced at his brothers, then at Dora Jones, who ran the hotel, and her friend Jean Campbell. Jean's eyes were wide, her mouth opening and closing like a fish.

"Are you two sure about this?" his brother Sterling asked.

Irving stepped forward, his arm around Sarah Crawford. "I've never been so sure about anything in my life."

1

"Mr. Darling's going to be my new daddy," Lacey Crawford said, grinning.

Everyone looked at the child, Wallis included. He blinked a few times. He knew his brother was attracted to the widow Crawford. Anyone could see it. But in the back of his mind, part of him (a big part) hoped Irving wouldn't fall in love as Sterling and Conrad had. But he did, and that meant ...

Five heads turned to Phileas, who was as wide-eyed as the women. He gulped, then stared at Irving. "What ... what will you do?"

Irving straightened and looked him in the eye. "I don't know."

Wallis gulped this time. If Irving, along with Sterling and Conrad, stayed, then Phileas would have to take over the family's title and estate back in England. He glanced at Dora. Phileas, once he got around to working on the hotel, would spend a lot of time with her. What if *he* fell hopelessly in love? Then again, this was Phileas, the artist of the family. He might not fall in love with Dora, but her hotel. His masterpiece. Egad, what a thought.

Wallis gulped again. If either happened, and Phileas stayed ...

"Congratulations." Sterling gave Irving a hug, then kissed Sarah on the cheek. "Well, I'm ... speechless."

Wallis gulped again, catching his older brother's attention.

Sterling smiled at him. "As you can see, we're all at a

loss for words, other than to say we wish you all happiness."

Phileas also kissed Sarah on the cheek, then smiled. "Welcome to the family."

She blushed. "Thank you, Phileas."

Oliver, the youngest brother, was standing halfway up the hotel's staircase. A skunk had sprayed him earlier that afternoon and he couldn't get too close to anyone. "Congratulations," he called to them.

"Thank you, brother," Irving called back.

"Well," Phileas said. "We should, um, celebrate." He smiled at Dora. "Do you need any help?"

Wallis gasped. The last thing he wanted was for Phileas to fall under love's spell. Being fifth in line to take over the title and estate, Wallis thought himself safe, and he wanted to keep things that way. He hoped Phileas would do his duty if Irving stayed in Apple Blossom.

Sterling, the oldest, was still on the fence about going back to England. Conrad had already decided. He was staying and he and Cassie were already making their wedding plans. Letty and Sterling were as well. If they married here, there was nothing Mother and Father could do if Sterling returned to England with a wife. They'd have to accept her.

Irving and Sarah, however, were another matter. She had two young children, Flint and Lacey. What would their parents do if Irving married and returned to England as a stepfather? Mother would be furious at first. The scandal would be widespread. Not that that sort of thing hadn't happened before, but Mother was funny that way.

He glanced at Phileas again. His brother was heading for the kitchen with Dora to help prepare something special. He didn't mind getting his hands dirty and Wallis smiled at the thought. Himself, he preferred the life they had in England and didn't fancy staying in America. But he also didn't want to return and take on the responsibility of a vast estate and that blasted title of Viscount Darlington. He'd not have a moment's peace!

Dash it all! He'd have to do something about it, but what? He couldn't come between Sterling and Letty, or any of the other couples. It would be wrong. But he could prevent Phileas from falling in love. The question was how?

He slipped into the lobby. Oliver was still on the stairs. The smell of skunk permeated the room. "Ollie, oh, dear ..."

"I'm sorry, but how do you think I feel?" He backed up the staircase a few steps. "I'll go to my room and read." He disappeared.

Wallis sighed. "Poor chap."

"Poor chap is right."

Wallis jumped. "Jean, goodness, you ..."

"Scared you? It's usually one of you that takes me or Dora by surprise." She glanced at the kitchen door. "Speaking of which, I should see if Dora needs any help."

"Yes, you should." His eyes suddenly lit up. "And ... might I have you send Phileas out here? After all, if you and Dora are both working in the kitchen, Phileas doesn't need to be there. I'm sure Irving has some things to discuss with the rest of us."

"Of course," Jean said. "I'll tell him now." She returned to the dining room.

Wallis exhaled and paced. What was he going to do? He couldn't keep using Jean to keep Phileas from Dora. She'd start asking questions, for one.

Then he smiled as an idea struck. "Yes, that's what I'll do."

"What?" Sterling asked as he came into the lobby.

"Oh, just thinking aloud." Wallis stopped pacing. "Are you joining us for dinner or are you off to Letty's?"

"Letty's. She'll want to hear about this." Sterling put a hand on Wallis' shoulder. "Wallis, I don't want you to worry."

He did his best not to laugh. Too late for that. "But you haven't decided."

"I'm close." Sterling smiled and left the lobby.

Wallis watched him go and shook his head. "Close to staying, you mean." More than Letty had enchanted Sterling's heart. Apple Blossom itself was getting under his skin.

Wallis went to the front counter and leaned against it. Little things kept cropping up in conversation that led him to believe that Sterling was becoming invested in the town. He wanted to make sure the new doctor, once he finally arrived, was a real physician and not some snake-oil salesman. The fact the doc was Agnes Featherstone's nephew had a lot to do with it. If Agnes could pinch a penny, she would. She also made sure she had her hand in everything in town, including who the new doctor would be.

He thought of Rev. Arnold. He would either retire soon or die of old age. Either way, he would have to be replaced, and Wallis wondered if Agnes didn't have someone in mind to fill that position too. But would the man want to take on the role of both preacher and schoolteacher as the old reverend had done?

It was too much to think about right now. He had to figure out a way to keep Phileas away from Dora.

"Brother," Phileas said as he strolled into the lobby. "Jean said you wanted to see me?"

"Oh, um, yes." Great, now think of something! "Uh, it's about Sarah's house. How soon do you think we can get the floor done?"

Phileas clasped his hands behind him. "Hmm, good question. Our timetable is growing smaller by the day. If it wasn't for the horrible stench ..."

"I know." He glanced at the staircase. "Poor Oliver."

Phileas nodded. "Yes, that brings it down to the five of us. Unless we figure out a way to work around him. He stinks something awful."

"That he does." Wallis paced again. "A few days, a week, what?"

"A day to tear it up with all of us working. A day, maybe two to put in the new floor, again, with all of us working. But that's providing we get the lumber in a timely manner. We need to speak to Woodrow Atkins. I know he brought a recent load to town."

"That's not so bad. Then what comes next?"

"Well, I'd like to start on the hotel ..."

"No!" Wallis shook his head. "I could ..."

"Yes?"

Wallis grinned. "Start on Jean's place. I'll need you."

Phileas cringed. "I say, there's not a lot to work with there. Have you seen her dwelling yet?"

"No, I've never been up to the living quarters."

"Considering the size of the um, funeral parlor, I don't think it's much." Phileas went to the front window of the hotel and looked out. "Irving and Sarah inspected the old millinery shop the other day. Irving wanted to see if it would suit her. If I know him, he'll talk her into buying it."

"That leaves her place empty." Wallis glanced at the kitchen. "It might suit Jean if her living quarters are next to nothing."

"If she bought Sarah's place," Phileas said. "She'd have plenty of room and it's close enough to walk to town."

Wallis smiled. "So you'll help me?"

Phileas sighed. "Oh, very well. A few more days away from the hotel won't hurt."

Wallis smiled in relief. So far, so good.

"What's happening to this town?" Dora asked. "First Letty, then Cassie, and now Sarah. Who knew love was so close?"

Ha! Jean made a face. "Close?" She began slicing an onion. "Maybe it was dumb luck."

Dora shook her head. "I don't know. None of our friends were looking for love."

Jean laughed. "That's because there's no place in Apple Blossom *to* look for it. Other than the captain, there are no single men, remember?"

Dora winked. "There are now."

Jean gasped. "You're not ..."

"No," Dora said with another shake of her head. "I was thinking about you."

"Me?" Jean thought of tossing an onion at her. She was the last person in town any of the Darlings would be interested in. After all, who wanted to woo an undertaker?

She got back to slicing as her heart sank. She tried not to think about it in the months following the "incident" but was thinking about it now. Letty, Cassie and Sarah had all found love with some of the Darlings. But not her. She would not allow herself to think about ...

"We'll have to make a wedding cake. Letty's will be first." Dora left the stove, came to the worktable and scooped onion slices into a bowl. "Between the two of us we can make some fine cakes."

Jean forced a smile. "I agree." She finished slicing and

brought the rest of the onions to the pot. "Here." She tossed them in. "I'll cut up the carrots next."

Dora smiled. "Thanks." She added some salt and pepper then gave the contents a stir. She was making vegetable beef soup. Jean gave Dora the recipe, and it was one of her favorites. She was sure the men would enjoy it.

Jean left the kitchen, went down the hall and out the back door. She'd pulled up carrots from Dora's garden and put them in the root cellar just yesterday, so they were still nice and fresh. She gathered the carrots and some potatoes and headed back to the kitchen. The celebration would start tonight and spread through town tomorrow if it hadn't already.

Jean brought the vegetables to the pump, washed them, then took them inside. As she cut them up, she thought of her life in Apple Blossom since the incident. She, like so many others, lost a family member—in her case, her father. Her mother died long ago and though she was lonely, she still had her friends. But those same friends were being whisked away, one by one, by a group of handsome Englishmen. Soon they'd be married, and where did that leave her?

Was she jealous? Well ...

But did it matter? Who would want her anyway? They'd not only get her, but the undertaker business as well. A job few people wanted. No one did after her father died, so she had to take things over and keep the business running. Only problem was, there had been no business for some time now. A big part of her didn't want there to be. She knew everyone in town and couldn't stand the thought of losing any of them. Every time she looked at Rev. Arnold, she cringed.

She put the vegetables in a bowl and left them on the worktable. "I'm heading back to my place while the soup's simmering."

"Go ahead," Dora said. "I can manage the biscuits." She stepped away from the stove, wiping her hands on her apron. "You're coming back."

Jean sighed and forced another smile. "Of course."

"Good." Dora picked up the bowl of vegetables and took it to the stove.

Jean slipped out the kitchen door into the hall. As she cut through the lobby, she picked up the faint smell of skunk and grimaced. Poor Oliver. She hoped the stench faded sooner than later. Maybe she could find a few books for him. At least he'd have something to do during his isolation.

Jean left the hotel, went home, and entered her little nest. She had a parlor/kitchen and a bedroom. She used to sleep downstairs in the storeroom on a cot and still thought of the tiny space as hers, though she'd had to share it with a neighboring cadaver on occasion. When that happened, she kept the door to the storeroom closed.

She went into the bedroom and looked around. The nightstand had a stack of books on it. Her other books were downstairs in her "old room". She had dozens of them and could do a lot of reading, even before Pa died.

Not a lot of folks passed in Apple Blossom before *it* happened.

She pushed the thought aside. She'd had to deal with more death than she wanted in the days following the ordeal. Mr. Atkins was kind enough to help her build coffins, and Captain Stanley helped with all the rest.

Jean sat on her bed with a sigh. She had the smallest living quarters in town, not to mention the smallest business. Pa had money set aside, but he'd done other things when he wasn't being the undertaker. He helped Mr. Atkins at his sawmill and did the same for Mr. Smythe come harvest time. In fact, Pa, more than anyone else, had taken charge of the apple orchards. All these things brought in extra money and kept the family fed.

Then Ma died, and it was just the two of them. Now with Pa gone, she wasn't sure how she was going to make the extra funds. She had enough to see her through the winter, but come spring if Alma at the general store raised her prices, she might not make it to summer. She had to find creative ways to make money or starve.

She looked around, her eyes settling on the stack of books on her nightstand. Of course! She could sell books. She'd read so many growing up, and was sure a lot of folks in town would love the stories as much as she did. Her collection consisted of a lot of classic tales. And after she began making money, she could order more books to sell. But first, she'd have to organize the books and figure out where to sell them. Alma might let her sell some in her store, but where would she put them?"

Her face lit up. No one was using the new town library. Maybe she could rent it. In fact, there were only a couple of small boxes with donated books in it. Hmmm, could she have a combination bookstore and library?

Jean pondered the possibilities as she tidied her little home. She could think of only one stumbling block. Agnes.

She sank onto the bed with a sigh. Agnes Featherstone would try to stop her before she got started. She considered herself the queen of Apple Blossom and tried to rule with an iron fist. Or, in Agnes' case, a rolling pin, which Jean imagined she waved at Mr. Featherstone whenever he disagreed with her. And that was probably more than anyone knew, at least behind closed doors.

"Maybe I should talk to Mr. Featherstone first." She nodded to herself and formed her plan. If he gave her permission to use the library, then Agnes couldn't make him renege, could she? Not that she wouldn't try. But Mr. Featherstone, despite being married to Agnes, was a kind soul who tried to do the right thing.

She smiled and looked at her stack. She'd take them downstairs, add them to the others, then as soon as she was through speaking to Mr. Featherstone, haul them over to the library.

But what if he said no?

She sighed again. "With my luck Agnes will turn me into the town librarian." Was it a paid position? She thought so, but what did a librarian make? The same as a teacher, or less? One of Pa's friends was a teacher, and she remembered them talking once before she and her family moved to Apple Blossom. He made forty-eight dollars annually. She winced at the thought. Yep. A librarian probably made less.

Jean took an armload of books downstairs, put them in the storeroom, then went to fetch the rest. She'd count them, see how many she had, then go across the street and peek through the library windows. She might need more shelves. As soon as Agnes got word that Irving and Sarah were in love, she'd ask Mr. Featherstone about the building. Hopefully Agnes would be too busy trying to find out what was going on with the Darlings to bother with her.

Chapter Two

Wallis went to his room, sat on the bed, and puzzled over his current predicament. If Phileas fell in love, he was doomed. The hotel would become his brother's masterpiece, and he might not want to leave it. He'd treat it like a child, something he could mold into what he wanted it to be. Dora would be an added benefit, and a pretty one at that.

Of course, he could be wrong and that's not what Phileas would do at all, but how to be sure? Phileas was first and foremost an artist, and they could be screwy.

Wallis picked up a book he'd purchased at Alma's store. He'd already read through the ones he brought for the trip, not to mention the ones his brothers brought. He'd have to buy a new one.

He left his room and headed for Alma's. He knew what she had in stock, and he was familiar with a lot of them. Still, he might find some literary nugget to sink his teeth into. At least it would take his mind off what was happening with his brothers. Drat love, anyway.

He came out of the hotel, saw Jean come out of the tiny funeral parlor, and noticed she carried several books. He met her in the middle of the street. "So, what are those?"

She looked at the books in her hands. "I was trying to estimate something."

"What?"

She nodded at the tiny library next to the hotel. "Shelf height. I have some enormous books."

He looked at the library. "But that's not open. It's never been, has it?"

"No. There were those preparing it, but ... they're no longer with us." She hung her head.

He bent down to catch her eye. "I understand."

She straightened. "Do you?"

"Yes. Here, let me help you." He took the books and carried them across the street. "So are you opening the library? I could do with a good book." He looked at the books in his hands. "*The Adventures of Huckleberry Finn, The Vanished Diamond, The Merry Adventures of Robin Hood.* Hmmm, these look good. Mind if I check one out?"

She sighed. "I was ... hoping to sell them."

"Oh, I see." He peeked at the titles again. "How much?"

Her eyes rounded. "You ... you want to buy them?"

"If they're for sale, yes." He studied her. Was she confused? "Jean? Is everything all right?"

She smiled. "Y-yes. I just didn't expect ..."

"To make a sale?"

She hung her head again. "I ... need the money."

He saw red creep into her cheeks and his heart went out to her. He glimpsed the tiny funeral parlor across the street. "Your place is so small. Do you own it?"

"Yes."

He nodded in understanding. "I don't suppose you've had much business since ..." He shrugged.

"No, I haven't." She headed for the library.

He hurried after her. "So you're looking for other sources of income?"

"Yes." She went onto the porch and peeked through the windows.

He did too. There were a few shelves but that was it. He spied some small stacks of books, probably donated by the townspeople. Her endeavor would not bring her much, poor thing. "Can Apple Blossom support a library?"

"I'm not sure. When we built it, we hadn't got that far. My father and a few others, including Alma's pa, thought to make it a free library. With donations, we could buy new books for it a few times a year."

"I see. But you'd like to turn it into a bookstore instead?"

She nodded but kept quiet. It had to be embarrassing to admit she needed the money.

"Aren't there other things you can do?"

Her eyes met his as she shrugged. "I can cook, but slaving over a hot stove all day doesn't appeal to me either."

"What about only part of the day?"

She glanced at the library window and back. "What do you mean?"

"You have something few do, Jean. Time. While you don't have funerals to take care of, you can work at so many things in between. Yes, there's this library, but if Sarah Crawford sells her place and buys the old millinery shop, there's talk of turning it into a bakery. You could work with her. I've heard it mentioned."

"Are you sure?"

He saw the hopefulness in her eyes. "Irving talked about it a few days ago. But if you'd rather wait for Sarah to approach you on the matter, then by all means, do."

She went to the library door and tried the handle. It was locked. "Mr. Featherstone has the key."

"He owns the building?"

"Yes."

"Shall we take a stroll?"

She stared at him a moment. "Stroll? Where?"

"To see Mr. Featherstone, of course."

She slowly smiled. "You'd come with me?"

"Of course. There's nothing wrong with what you're doing. But if Agnes is there ..."

She nodded sagely. "She's a handful, no doubt about

17

it. I can't stand the way she badgers people to get what she wants. She tries to run the whole town."

"I've noticed," he said with a smile. "Which is why I'm offering my moral support."

She bit her lip and forced a smiled. "You must think me weak."

"Not at all." He looked her over. "Meek. Kind and generous, but not weak."

She blushed. "I feel weak." Her eyes filled with a sadness he couldn't comprehend. But then, he'd lost no one close to him before. Like Letty, Cassie, and Sarah, Jean was all alone in the world save the company of a few friends, all of which were about to marry his brothers.

"Come," he said. "Let's go speak with Mr. Featherstone."

She set the books on a bench by the door, and they were off. "How do you feel about your brothers falling in love?"

He took a deep breath. "I ... I'm torn. Phileas, Oliver, and I are losing them." He stopped and faced her. "Not only to love, but to Apple Blossom."

She looked up the street. "And that's a bad thing?"

"It is if you're the one leaving your brothers behind. Home will never be the same without them."

Her eyes filled with sympathy. "I'm sorry."

Wallis shook his head. "Don't be. We're happy for our brothers, the three of us. And we've gained sisters. But I dare say, I can't stand the thought of losing another. If Phileas were to fall in love ... I shudder to think what our poor parents will do."

She gave him another sympathetic look. "It would devastate them?"

"Yes, but with Phileas, it's not Dora he would fall in love with, but the hotel."

She blinked a few times. "What?"

He nodded. "You've seen what he can do?"

"Yes, I saw Cassie's place, and Letty's. I haven't seen Sarah's yet. I know it's not finished."

"Indeed not." He stared at the buildings across the street. "Phileas is liable to let that hotel woo him into staying once he works on it."

"That's ... odd," she stated.

"Not at all. Artists, actors, writers, they're all a bit ... different."

She smiled. "You're saying your brother is strange."

Wallis shrugged. "I don't want to see him throw his future away." Or his, but he wasn't going to tell her that. In fact, he shouldn't be telling her this to begin with, but talking about it helped him process things.

"Well, if that's how you feel, then give him something he can work on at home in England."

"Yes, but what?" He turned to Dora's hotel. "That building is like an evil temptress. Once he starts working on it, he may never stop."

She shrugged. "Like I said, give him something else to work on."

Wallis nodded. "You're right, but ..." His eyes lit up.

He didn't have to give Phileas a building or decorating project at home. The point was to just get him there. If Phileas thought another of their company was falling in love (namely, him), perhaps he'd step forward to take over the estate and title after Father passed. Oliver, the youngest, was the least equipped to take things over. Phileas knew this and also knew he would be the logical choice at that point.

"What is it?" Jean asked.

He smiled at her. How to explain things? "I think I have an idea. But I'll need your help."

"What is it?"

He smiled. "Well, to keep Phileas from falling in love with the hotel, he needs, as you said, something else to keep his mind occupied, something that will make him want to return home."

"And that would be?" She eyed the bank up the street.

He'd better make this quick. He looked her in the eyes. "Jean, would you consider, allowing me to court you?"

Her eyes widened. "What?"

"Not for real, just long enough to make Phileas realize he needs to return to England with Oliver and me."

She stepped back, a shocked look on her face. "Are you serious?"

"It wouldn't be for long." Heat crept into his cheeks.

"Letty and Sterling pretended to court at first, when in reality they were already in love."

Her jaw dropped. "They're getting married, everyone in town knows it."

"Yes, but in the beginning ... oh, never mind. Suffice to say, if it looks like I'm falling in love with you, then Phileas will see how important it is for him to return to England."

"But you're going back too."

"I am, which means I'll throw you over shortly before we leave."

She rolled her eyes. "Oh, golly, thanks."

"Since we won't really be in love, what does it matter? Will you help me?"

Her eyes narrowed. "It'll never work."

"It will if we make things look convincing. And we don't have to be together all the time to do it. We see each other often enough already. Nothing has to change."

"What about your other brothers?"

"Ah, yes," he said and rubbed his chin. "The others." Wallis shrugged "They need not know either. I could test the waters, as they say."

She shook her head. "I still don't know."

He closed the distance between them. "Think about it?"

She laughed. "And you think your brother is odd?"

He shrugged helplessly. Either she'd help him or not.

Her shoulders slumped. "I'll think about it."

"Splendid," he said with a smile. "Now what say we

speak to Mr. Featherstone about that library?" He offered his arm.

Jean looked at it, arched an eyebrow, then looped her arm through his.

Wallis smiled again as they continued down the street. No sense wasting time with their ruse. Let folks see her on his arm. With any luck, they'd think their courtship had begun.

"You want to do what?" Francis Featherstone asked. "Run the library?"

"As it's the town library," Wallis said. "I would think it a paid position?"

Mr. Featherstone scratched his head and rose from his chair. "A moment." He craned his neck to see out his office door. Thank goodness Agnes wasn't in the bank when they arrived. If Jean's guess was right, Mr. Featherstone was making sure she still wasn't. He tiptoed to the door and closed it. "Now, you were saying?"

Jean gave Wallis a sidelong glance and smiled. "I'd like to open the library and work in it."

"This town needs the establishment," Wallis added. "Reading is important."

"To those that can," Mr. Featherstone agreed. "And I think it a fine idea. If not for the, um, incident, it would be open now."

"Then I can do it?" Jean asked.

"What about your business?"

She noted he didn't say undertaker. "When have I had any?"

He sat. "Fair point." Mr. Featherstone drummed his fingers on the desktop. "Jean, I like the idea, but a paid position?"

"Paid by the town, of course," Wallis said. "That's how libraries work."

"Donations, maybe ..." Mr. Featherstone hedged.

She sighed. "Agnes doesn't want to pay anyone, does she? It's why she wanted everything done through donations."

Mr. Featherstone cringed and nodded.

She sank a little in her chair. "Why am I not surprised?"

"Say donations ran it," Wallis said. "But Jean was still the librarian. That would entitle her to those donations for her pay."

"Well, I suppose ..." Mr. Featherstone said. "But as the official librarian, you'd have to keep the place up. Order the books and pay for them out of those same donations." He gave her a firm nod.

"So I can open the library?" she asked. For all she knew, she'd make more in donations to live on than what Agnes would have the town pay her.

"You may," Mr. Featherstone said. "But give me your estimates for the cost of books and shelving. Again, you'll have to rely on donations to see it all done, including your pay."

"Would she have to give anything to the town treasury?" Wallis asked. "Considering she's doing all the work and not being paid out of the treasury, I would think not."

"That's right," Mr. Featherstone said. "The town can't afford to pay you, Miss Campbell, but if you can keep the place in good working order and maintain it with the donations, then do so and with my blessing."

She grinned. "Thank you, Mr. Featherstone. Thank you!" She left her chair, went around the desk and hugged him.

He blushed to his toes and smiled. "You're welcome. Now run along, my dear." He waved them toward the door.

Wallis gave him a parting smile, then ushered her that way. She could hardly believe it!

"Oh, Miss Campbell?"

She turned around. "Yes, Mr. Featherstone?"

He opened a drawer and held up a key.

"Oh, yes." She crossed the room and took it. "Thank you."

"My pleasure."

With a parting smile, she left the office. In the bank, Agnes sat at a desk and eyed them as they left. As soon as they reached the door, Jean watched her march into her husband's office. "Let's go before she ruins everything."

Wallis looked over his shoulder as the door to Mr. Featherstone's office closed. "She wouldn't."

"She would." She pulled him outside. "Let's get to the library and see what I've gotten myself into."

They headed down the boardwalk, but not before hearing a muffled screech come from inside the bank. Jean sighed. "He just told her. We'd better hurry." She picked up the pace and by the time they were passing the saloon, heard her name called from somewhere behind them. "Miss Campbell!" She kept going.

"Shouldn't we stop?" Wallis asked.

"No."

"But ..."

She pulled him along and walked faster.

"Miss Campbell!" Agnes yelled. "Come back here."

Jean rolled her eyes. "Oh, very well." She turned on her heel and glared at Agnes.

She was not only glaring back but looked like a charging bull as she stomped toward them.

"Great Scott," Wallis said. "I've never seen the like."

"Pray you never do again," she said dryly. "Brace yourself."

He looked suitably panicked. "What?"

She crossed her arms. "Here it comes ..."

"Jean Campbell!" Agnes bellowed when she reached them. "What's this I hear about you opening and running the library?"

Her arms still crossed, she looked Agnes in the eyes. "Someone has to do it."

"Well, of course, and it's about time someone did."

Her arms dropped. "What?"

"If you want to volunteer at the library, there's nothing wrong with that. But all proceeds will go to the bank."

"Excuse me," Wallis said. "That's not what Mr. Featherstone just agreed to."

"I don't care what Francis told you," Agnes spat. "She can work in the library and take care of it, but she'll not make a penny. It's strictly a volunteer position."

Jean crossed her arms again. "Mr. Featherstone already stated what's to be done. I will take care of the library and all it entails, including maintaining the building and grounds. It will run on donations out of which I'll be paid."

Agnes seethed. Jean didn't know anyone could turn such a brilliant shade of red. "We'll see about that." She turned on her heel and stormed back to the bank.

Jean heaved a sigh. "Well, so much for that idea. She'll badger Mr. Featherstone into getting her way."

"It's not right," Wallis said.

"No, but what's to be done about it?" She started down the boardwalk again. "Agnes runs this town, and that's that."

"Jean," he said and took her by the arm. "Don't let her bully you. She can't do anything, not really. Not if the town votes on how the library should be run."

She was speechless for a moment. "Really?"

"Of course. The library belongs to the town, not to Agnes."

She thought a moment. "It was volunteers that built it. Everyone donated work, materials, the books."

"Exactly. Agnes is just being greedy." He smiled and motioned her forward. They walked the rest of the way and stood before the library door. Wallis unlocked it, smiled warmly and ushered her inside. "My, will you look at this place?"

She did. It had been so long since she was in here, she'd forgotten what was done. There was a potbellied stove at the rear of the one-room building. They had placed a desk in one corner, a couple of old chairs and a small table in the other. One shelving unit (compliments of Mr. Atkins) graced the center of the room. One wall had another set of shelves. The opposite side of the room had none. "There's plenty of room," she commented.

"Indeed." Wallis looked around. "And room for more shelves and perhaps a table or two." He smiled at her. "Who were the volunteers?"

"Half the town. It would have opened sooner if not for …" She looked at the floor.

He tucked a finger under her chin and brought her face up. "Everyone that worked on this, even the ones no longer here, would be proud to see it open. In fact, we should dedicate the library to them. Don't you think?"

Her eyes misted. "Oh, Wallis." Without thinking, she hugged him.

To her surprise, he hugged her back. "There, there. Chin up. You have a lot of work to do."

She drew back. "I'm sorry, I …"

He smiled again. "As one book lover to another, I'd like to help."

She smiled back. "You would?"

Wallis nodded. "I must spend some time on Sarah's house, but I can also spare some for this place. Between the two of us, we could have it up and running in no time."

Jean smiled then remembered what he'd asked her earlier. "Oh, but ... are you helping because you want to? Or because of Phileas?"

"Well, if my brother sees us spending time together working on this place, and comes to his own conclusions, then we wouldn't have to pretend anything, would we?"

She gave him a knowing look. "That would be preferable."

Wallis looked sheepish, but nodded.

Jean went outside to retrieve the books she left on the library's bench. She'd let Wallis help all he wanted. But to pretend they were courting? She wasn't so sure about that.

Chapter Three

Wallis measured the library shelves and figured out how much lumber and materials he would need. They could have shelves lining both walls of the building, with two more sets in the center. "We could put more chairs near the front windows, unless you want to put in more shelving."

Jean eyed the space. "Why more chairs?"

He went to the front of the library, arms held wide.

"What are you doing?" she asked.

"Measuring. After a fashion." He gave her a grin. "Comfortable chairs, and maybe a little table for a lamp."

"But why?" Her hands went to her hips as she cocked her head.

"For reading, what else?"

"Oh, I hadn't thought of that. I figured people would check out a book, then take it home and read it."

"True, but wouldn't it be nice to cozy up by the stove and read one here? It would be peaceful, for one." He went to the shelves at the wall. "I enjoy being with books. We have a library at home ..."

"You do?" Her eyes lit up. "Does your town library have tables and chairs?"

He tried not to look guilty. He was speaking of his family's house library. "Yes. And it's larger than this one." Indeed, twice as large and with an immense fireplace and rich furnishings.

She sighed. "You're right, that would be nice. Maybe someone has a few old chairs they could donate."

He smiled and closed the distance between them. "You could read to the children in town."

"Or Captain Stanley could." She went to the corner by one of the front windows. "Maybe here?"

"Or closer to the stove in colder months." He headed for the other end of the building. The space was about thirty-five feet long and twenty wide. It wouldn't take much to build the shelves and fix the place up. He could make a donation for new books and, as the town grew, others could do the same. "Young families," he mused aloud.

"What?" Jean asked as she strolled his way.

"Apple Blossom needs more young families. Just think of what the town could become?" He went to the stove and looked it over. It was brand new. Good. He turned around and smiled at her. "Can you imagine it?"

She shrugged. "I don't know. I've never thought of

the town growing. Apple Blossom is out of the way. And it's a half day's ride to Virginia City. Most folks would rather settle there. They have all they need in one place."

"But look at how beautiful this place is, Jean." He took her hand and went to the front of the library. "A charming little town surrounded by apple orchards. With a little ingenuity, a handful of people could make this place into something special."

"Special? Apple Blossom? How?"

He laughed. "With apples, of course. You have acres of them."

She ran a finger over the wood of a windowpane. "Yes, but who would travel out of their way for apple pie or cider?"

"How about folks in Virginia City and Bozeman? You could start with an annual event like a … a …" He grinned. "… an apple festival."

She gazed out the window and looked to be thinking about it.

"The whole town could get involved," he went on. "You could have games, prizes, different things to sell."

She glanced at him. "You mean apples."

"In different forms, yes, but as you're the only ones around for miles with any, take advantage of that."

She headed for the other end of the building, took the chair by the stove and sat.

Wallis studied her. "What are you doing?"

"I'm trying to imagine this place filled with books. There would be people walking by outside, going about their business, and then Dora would come through that door asking for my help because she has so many guests in the hotel because of the town's apple festival, she can't serve them all."

"Ah, yes," he said with a wag of his finger. "But only because her hired help is off running an errand for her." He smiled. "To the train station, to pick up supplies Dora ordered."

Jean smiled back. "Such nice thoughts."

"Realistic ones," he added.

She left the chair. "Do you think so?" She looked around and ran a hand down the bodice of her dress. It was a pale yellow with tiny flowers all over it. There was no lace or any other sort of frippery, just some small white buttons down the front. She was pretty, and he realized she had the warmest brown eyes he had ever seen. She also looked troubled.

"Things can be done, Jean," he reassured. "Lots of things. Apple Blossom needs a little nudge to get things started, that's all."

"Nudge?" She laughed. "To bring people here?"

"Yes." He stood behind the other chair and rested his hands on it. "The new doctor will be here soon. That's always a good thing. A lot of folks won't settle in a town that doesn't have one."

"Or a schoolhouse," she pointed out.

"Yes, there's that." He went around the chair and sat. "This place could use a café of some sort too."

She paced. "But who would run it?"

"You're a wonderful cook."

She stopped in front of him and laughed. "But I have the library, remember?"

Wallis rubbed his chin a few times. He didn't know why, but all this talk of improving the town, was getting him excited. He always loved a project. But he'd have to settle for helping Jean with the library and fixing up her place. Speaking of which ... "Ahem. Um, how's your house? You mentioned last week it could use a few things."

"My place? Well, yes, but I can take care of them. Really, why bother?"

"I'd like to look at it, anyway. Since I'm helping with the library, I might as well help with that too. You are on our list."

She sighed. "Ah, yes, the list. So far, every house you've work on has gained ..." She smiled. "I'm not sure what to call it."

"Love?"

"I was thinking a husband. But no one's gotten themselves hitched yet." She took a sudden interest in the stovepipe.

"Yes. But we both know they will." He went to her. "Jean, think about what can be done with the library and your place. By the way, when can I see it?"

She cringed. "You really want to?"

"Of course."

She sighed. "Okay, but don't judge me."

Wallis smiled. "Come now, it can't be that bad. Have you seen Sarah's place?"

"Many times. My place is like that, only much smaller."

His heart went out to her. He couldn't imagine living in such a tiny structure. The rooms in the manor house, including the library, were huge. "How small?"

She looked around. "About half the size of this."

He tried not to wince. "Less space, less to fix. Let's have a look." He started to usher her toward the door.

She took one last look at the shelves and books and went outside. After locking up they crossed the street to the undertaker's. It was next to the livery stable. On the other side of the small building was an empty lot, then the general store. Wallis tried to imagine what sort of business could be put in the space. A post office, perhaps? On the other side of the general store was another empty building, and he wondered who had occupied it.

They reached the small two-story building. "The funeral parlor is on the first floor." She went inside. "As you can see, there's not much here."

Wallis studied the room. It was only twenty feet from front to back, and maybe twelve feet wide. There was a narrow staircase toward the back. "Your living quarters?"

She nodded at the ceiling.

He looked around some more. There was a potbellied stove, also near the back, and a desk and chair.

Coffins took the rest of the space up. "What's through that door?"

She went to the door near the staircase. "A storeroom." She opened it. "I stored my books in here."

He looked inside. There were a few crates, several stacks of books, a small barrel or two, and a thin rolled-up mattress. He pointed at it. "What's that for?"

She went crimson. "I ... used to sleep in here." She nodded at one corner of the little room. "Over there. My parents had the bedroom upstairs."

His heart pinched. "I see." So she took over the bedroom after the outlaws killed her father. "Do you need more storage?"

"No. This has always served. But you have to remember, I have little business."

He smiled. "That's a good thing. Besides, you're going to have a library to run." He headed for the stairs. "May I?"

She nodded and started up the stairs.

He could only imagine what her living quarters were like and was already cringing.

At the top of the stairs was a little landing. She opened the door and went through. "Oh, dear," Wallis said.

"Yes, I know. It's small."

He took in the tiny cookstove, dry sink, and hutch. There was also a table, two chairs, and a worn settee in front of the window. There was a door near the hutch. "Bedroom?"

She nodded without a word.

He opened it. A bed, a dresser, and a washstand. That was it. Really, you couldn't fit anything else in there. "Right, then." He went to the windows and looked across the street at the library. "Have you ... any money saved?"

"What?" she asked, breathless.

Wallis faced her. "Money? Have you any? Enough to, say, buy Sarah Crawford's place?"

Jean gasped. "I ... no." She shook her head and laughed. "I'm sorry, but no."

Wallis smiled gently. The poor thing, how could she survive? "I see. Well, we need to put our heads together, don't we?"

"And do what?"

"Think of a way for you to make a decent living."

Jean did her best not to take offense. Wallis was only trying to help, and the fact was, she needed to figure something out. If Agnes had her way, she'd be taking care of the library for free. "Yes," she finally said. "But what?"

He pursed his lips, his mouth twisting to one side, then the other.

She smiled. "Do you have something in your teeth?"

Wallis chuckled. "No, I tend to make a lot of faces while I'm thinking." He went to the table and sat. "I want to help you, Jean. Will you let me?"

"I ..." She was going to say yes, but her pride kicked in. "I'm not as pathetic as it seems."

"Don't say that," he scolded. "After what happened to this town, it threw a lot of people off course."

"The captain would say blown off, but I know what you mean. And yes, unfortunately I'm one of them." She went to the other chair and flopped into it. "Don't think I haven't tried to come up with something. So far books have been it."

He nodded. "A good idea, but there are variables we must consider."

She gave him a knowing smile. "Agnes."

"That's only one," he pointed out.

"Isn't she enough?" She left her chair. "Would you like some coffee?"

"Love some." He steepled his fingers and eyed her. "Can you sew?"

"Yes, but I'm not very good. Not like Cassie or Sarah." She went to the stove. "The dressmaker's shop is empty. The woman who ran it left like so many others." She got to work on the coffee. "Which brings up another point."

"Which is?"

She spooned coffee she ground that morning into the pot. "No one comes this way anymore. Yes, Apple Blossom is charming, beautiful in fact. But that's not its reputation anymore, not that it had one to begin with. All folks know about us now is that our town has been filled with ..." She turned around. "... death."

He looked sympathetic. "And you had to deal with your share of it, didn't you, being the daughter of the undertaker?"

She shrugged and turned back to the stove. "I wasn't the only one. But I had help, thank goodness. Mr. Atkins and the captain."

He smiled. "Thank Heaven for Captain Stanley. I notice he helps quite a few folks in town."

"That he does." She put the lid on the pot. The coffee she was using was for tomorrow morning. But that was all right. She had a guest after all. She went to the hutch, took out the cookie jar and set it on the table. "I have a few left if you'd like one."

He took off the lid. "Don't mind if I do."

She watched him bite into a sugar cookie, then returned to the stove. Like the rest of the Darlings, Wallis was handsome, but more boyish. No, that wasn't right. Bookish? She smiled. That fit. "What do you like to read?" She busied herself getting cups and saucers from the hutch.

"All kinds of things. Adventure stories, real adventures. Diaries of explorers, that sort of thing. It's one reason I was looking forward to this trip."

Her heart stilled. "And then you came here. And your trip ended."

He left the table. "No, it's not like that. If we had wanted to move on, we'd have done it. You and others in this town need help. We couldn't turn our backs on you."

She slowly turned around and faced him. "But you will leave. The question is, who is going with you?"

Wallis heaved a sigh. "Perhaps a few of the townspeople will be."

"Oh, dear, I ... I'd hate to think of Letty, Cassie and Sarah leaving Apple Blossom."

"And what about Dora?"

She gasped. "Oh, no, not Dora!"

He returned to his chair, sat, and crossed his arms. "Could happen."

Jean gasped again. "What are you talking about?"

He examined a fingernail. "Phileas."

"Your brother? What has he got to do with ... oh." Her eyes went wide. "Oh!"

He nodded. "There's a possibility that my brother could fall in love with more than the hotel."

Her hands went to her face. "Oh!"

"Indeed." He drummed his fingers on the tabletop. "It's a problem."

"For both of us." She began to pace. "I understand your frustration if Phileas stayed for that silly hotel. But if he married Dora and took her back to England ... I'd be all alone, my friends gone."

Wallis made a face. "And we can't let that happen."

She stared at him. Why did he look guilty? But he was right. "No, we can't. But there's nothing we can do about it if they fall for each other."

"Unless ..." He smiled.

"What?" He wasn't going to bring up that whole courting thing again, was he?

"If ..." He tapped the table. "... we were thought to be courting ..."

She pinched the bridge of her nose. "Not that."

"Just let them think it for a time. Phileas will be so busy trying to break us up, he won't have time to pay attention to Dora. Or she him."

She lowered her hand. He had a point. She knew Dora, and if she thought for a minute, she was falling in love with Wallis, Dora would be hounding her to find out what was going on. What could it hurt to let her think they were interested in each other for a few days? "Hmm, it might work." She went to the table and sat. "But Dora loves that hotel. And if Phileas could help her with it, she'd be so happy."

"And he will, but it would be better if all of us help him, and her. To leave the two of them with all the work, they'd be together constantly and look what happened to the others."

Now *she* made a face. "You're right. But even if Dora fell in love with Phileas, I don't think she'd ever leave Apple Blossom."

"Perhaps. Then my poor mother would be heartbroken." He put a hand over his heart for emphasis. "What a tragedy."

She narrowed her eyes. He was reminding her of an actor in a bad play. "You're being dramatic."

"And why not? It's bad enough three of my brothers

may not be going home with me. But a fourth would be too much."

She shouldn't. She *really* shouldn't. But he was willing to help her with the library ... "Very well, I'll help you."

His face lit up. "You will? Jolly good."

Jean took a cookie from the jar. "But only for a time." She took a generous bite and chewed. After a few days, the whole town would think they were courting and then what?

She watched Wallis take another cookie, noted his cheerful smile and tried not to smile herself. Part of her thought it a grand idea. It would be nice to be courted by someone, even if it was pretend. Apple Blossom wasn't growing and might not do so for years. She was facing spinsterhood and knew it. Why not have a few days of enjoyment, just to see what it would be like?

She brought some sugar to the table. "Will we ... hold hands?"

"Occasionally."

"Walk arm in arm down the street? Sit together in church?"

"Naturally."

She watched him chew, then checked the coffee. "And what about the rest of your brothers? What will they think?"

"The same thing Phileas will, I should hope." He mocked a scream. "Arghhhh! Wallis and Jean are courting!"

She giggled. "And the town?"

This time he frowned. "Did you hear that Wallis Darling and Jean Campbell are courting?" he hissed.

She laughed. "That's perfect! I don't think Mr. Featherstone would know the difference."

He laughed. "I don't look at things like Agnes."

"No, but that was an excellent imitation."

When the coffee was done, she filled their cups, and they chatted about the town, England, and of course the upcoming weddings.

Jean ran a finger over the rim of her cup. "You know, there might be one problem no one has thought of."

"Problem?" He sipped his coffee. "What are you talking about?"

"Rev. Arnold. He's so old and ... Mrs. Arnold is thinking of taking him to Bozeman."

His face fell. "What?"

"Yes, I just heard it yesterday. She spoke to Captain Stanley about taking them. They have doctors there, and ..."

He held up a hand. "Say no more." He took another sip and she could tell he was thinking.

"That means the town will be without a preacher too," she added.

He rolled his eyes. "I've no doubt Agnes will try to fill the position with another of her relatives."

"I don't think any of them are clergy." Of course, she hadn't known any of Agnes's relatives were doctors either, yet one was coming.

Wallis drained his cup and wiped crumbs from his face with a napkin. "So, the town needs several things, including a new preacher. I dare say, I hope Sterling has considered Rev. Arnold's condition."

She thought of Letty, Cassie and Sarah. She didn't know the latter as well as she did Cassie and Letty. Still, all three would be disappointed if Rev. Arnold wasn't able to marry them. Would he marry them all at once then?

Wallis got to his feet. "I must be going. I'll speak to the others about building some shelves for the library. I'll also return and take a better look at this place. For now, I must speak with Irving about Sarah's home. We need to tear up the floor in the bedroom."

"Yes, I know. Thank you for looking at the library with me and speaking to Mr. Featherstone. It was nice having support."

Wallis smiled warmly. "It was my pleasure." He put on his hat, and Jean showed him to the door. As soon as he left, she went to the table, refilled her cup, and sat. When all was said and done, what had she gotten herself into?

Chapter Four

Wallis joined Sterling and Irving at their usual table in the hotel dining room. There was no sign of the others. "Where is everyone?"

"Conrad and Phileas are speaking to Woodrow Atkins about getting more lumber," Sterling said. "We need to speed things up."

Wallis straightened in his chair. "Because?"

"Don't you want to get home?" Sterling asked.

He did, and with as many of his brothers along as possible. "What about the hotel and the other homes we were going to work on?"

Irving sighed. "That's what we're trying to figure out." He glanced at Sterling. "Among other things."

Wallis sighed too, his eyes flicking between them. He didn't get nervous, but the closer they got to their departure date, the antsier he became. With his luck, the only ones heading back to England would be Oliver and himself. "What things?"

"It's been brought to our attention that Rev. Arnold isn't doing well," Irving said.

"Who told you that?"

Sterling shrugged. "Rev. Arnold."

Wallis jerked back in his chair. "What?" Not that he didn't already know, Jean had just told him, but did this mean Sterling, Conrad and Irving would get married sooner rather than later?

"I'll speak to Captain Stanley after dinner," Sterling said. "Mrs. Arnold wants him to take them to Bozeman."

"Why not take the stage?" Wallis asked.

"Mrs. Arnold feels it would be too rough on him," Sterling said. "Captain Stanley can make the trip more comfortable."

Wallis sat back. "Dear me. The poor man."

Sterling nodded. "This means the town will need a new preacher. I'm going to ask the captain if he can find someone in Bozeman."

Wallis gaped at him. "How will he do that? Walk up to someone, hope they can handle the job, and drag them back here?"

Sterling shrugged. "He can at least put the word out."

Wallis wasn't sure what to think about this. On the one hand, his brothers couldn't get married without a preacher. But on the other, he wasn't sure how that would affect everything else going on. Who said any of his besotted brothers had to get married before he and the others left for home? That included Phileas. What if he got it in his head to stay behind for the hotel or ... gulp ... Dora?

Even if he didn't develop feelings for Dora, given enough time and money, Phileas could rebuild the entire hotel. Egad, what a thought. And if the idea somehow wormed its way into Phileas' head, then he'd never go home. Wallis could hear Mother screaming at him now.

Then Wallis had another horrible thought. What if Oliver stayed because the others were? Then he'd be stuck with everything. The title, the estate, Mother. Oh, the pain ...

"Wallis?" Irving said. "Are you all right? You've gone pale."

He gulped. "Perfectly fine."

Sterling peered at him. "You sure?"

He nodded, his mouth shut tight. He didn't dare voice any of this. Besides, Sterling and Irving were in love. They'd tell him he was overreacting and to keep a stiff upper lip. The estate would be in excellent hands, even if they were his.

Conrad waltzed into the dining room. "Sorry I'm late."

"You missed it," Sterling said. "I'll fill you in while we're eating."

"And Phileas," Wallis put in. "We can send a note to Ollie."

Conrad snorted. "Poor sot."

Irving tried to keep a straight face and couldn't manage it.

Wallis had too much on his mind to laugh. Instead he blurted, "Jean is going to run the library."

Everyone looked at him. "Library?" Conrad said.

"Yes, she spoke with Mr. Featherstone about it, and we looked to see what she'd need to get it going."

"Well," Irving said with a smile. "That's good news. The children in town would benefit from a library."

Wallis nodded. Of course Irving would think so, now that he was about to become a father to Lacey and Flint.

"Is it a volunteer position?" Sterling asked.

Wallis frowned. "If Agnes has her way, it will be. But Mr. Featherstone told Jean she could collect donations for books, maintenance and of course, some pay. She ... needs something. Thank goodness, she's had no business. But that also means no money."

"You're right," Sterling said. "Irving, didn't you suggest to Sarah ... oh, wait." He smiled. "Never mind."

"What?" Wallis said.

Irving smiled then shrugged. "I don't mind telling anyone now. You might remember I suggested to Sarah that she buy the old millinery and turn it into some sort of business she and Jean could run."

Wallis looked at each brother. Of course, he knew about it. But Conrad looked lost. "And?"

Irving smiled again. "I bought the building for her."

"What?!"

He nodded. "She could still turn it into a business. Dressmaking, sewing, baking. We'll live upstairs."

Everything went quiet.

Wallis had to remember to breathe. "You're ... staying?"

"I did just buy the building. Sarah should have the chance to make something of it."

"He's staying for now," Sterling said.

Wallis and Conrad's heads whipped around to him. "And what about you?" Conrad asked. "Have you decided what you're going to do?"

Sterling sighed and shook his head.

All eyes gravitated to Wallis. He stared back. "If ... if all three of you stay ..."

"Then Phileas is the one to take over," Sterling said.

Not that he had to say it. Wallis and everyone else at the table knew it would fall to Phileas. What no one was saying was that their brother was nowhere in sight. And when he was missing, he was usually with Dora.

Wallis' nose twitched. "I'll be helping Jean with the library and her place." His eyes skipped around the table. "When are we doing the floor at Sarah's?"

"We can tear the old floor out tomorrow," Sterling said. "If we start early enough, we can get done in time for you to spend a few hours with Jean."

"Good." He sat back. Should he say anything else? He cleared his throat. "Jean's rather attractive, don't you think?"

Silence again. Irving exchanged a look with Sterling

who exchanged one with Conrad. "Quite," Conrad said. "Are you looking forward to working on her place?"

He rested his hands on the table. He had their attention now. "She needs help. I plan to do what I can."

"What kind of help?" Sterling asked.

"She needs to support herself. The library will help, but she needs more. And her place ..." he shook his head. "There's nothing to it. She'd do well with Sarah's house."

Irving sighed. "Does she have money to buy it?"

"No." He stared at the table. He was telling them Jean's private business, but figured it wasn't anything folks in town didn't already know. "Like Sarah, she's in a bad way but doesn't act it."

"Oh, dear," Irving said. "Let me speak to Sarah. If Jean has a source of income, perhaps she could rent the house? It's the closest one to town and would give her plenty of room."

"I'd appreciate that, brother," Wallis said. "Thank you."

Irving nodded. "Any other business? Conrad?"

"None," he said. "Other than I'm staying. You all realize that."

"We do," Sterling said. "Irving, are you sure?"

He slowly nodded. "I think Sarah can do a lot with the old millinery. I must let her try."

Sterling drew in a breath. "Of course."

Silence descended on them like a cloud. They all knew what the others were thinking. If Sterling went home to England, the rest of them were free to live their lives as they saw fit. It was the advantage of being the second, third, fourth son and so on. But to be saddled with the title and estate was a tremendous responsibility. You lived for the estate, not for yourself.

Sterling was born to it. As the eldest, it was his responsibility to take it over. But nothing said he *had* to. With six sons, their father knew everything would be taken care of when he passed on.

Wallis fought against a shudder. He'd always wanted to travel, to see some of the wonderful things he'd read about in his family's library. Coming to America was part of that. But there were other places he'd love to see: India, Africa, parts of South America. All he saw now was his dream dwindling away, brother by brother, until there was only Oliver and him left untethered by love.

"Where is Phileas?" Conrad asked.

Wallis fought an eye roll. He was probably with Dora. "Has anyone checked the kitchen?"

"I'll do it." Sterling left his chair.

Irving glared at Wallis. "So you've noticed Jean, have you?"

He looked at him, suddenly at a loss for words. But here was his chance to plant seeds about his and Jean's fake courtship. "Um. Yes."

Conrad smiled. "You don't sound very enthusiastic."

Wallis tried to be casual and instead bit his lip to keep his jaw from moving back and forth. "She's ... well ... she likes books. I like books. Everyone knows that."

His brothers exchanged a look. "And I like pheasant,"

Irving said. "I haven't the foggiest idea if Sarah does." He smiled and leaned his way. "But tell me, what is it you and Jean have in common?"

"Other than books," Conrad added.

Wallis drew his upper lip into his mouth with his teeth. "Growing Apple Blossom."

His brothers' eyebrows shot to the ceiling. "What?" Irving said. "Did I hear you right?"

"As in, have people come to live here?" Conrad asked. "Yes."

Conrad smiled. "Well, well. Seems our brother has found himself a project."

Irving nodded as he eyed Wallis. "And not just improvements to Jean's humble abode."

All right, time to put on a show. "Little is right. Her place could fit in this room three times over. It's appalling it's so small. And to think she lived there with her parents." He slapped a hand on the table. "Did she tell you she slept downstairs in a storeroom on a little mattress?"

Irving and Conrad looked at each other and shrugged. "Can't say that she did," Conrad said.

"Well, it's true. The poor thing needs space. How can anyone thrive in such a ... a prison?"

They exchanged another look. "And I suppose you're going to break her out of it?" Irving asked.

"If it is within my power, yes." Wallis stood, tugged on his jacket, then marched toward the lobby. Let them chew on that. He tried not to chuckle as he hurried upstairs. He'd check on Oliver, then wander back down when it was time to eat. If his guess was right, that would be soon. Then he'd have to answer a barrage of questions about Jean. Most of which might come from Dora.

He rubbed his hands together. His little plan was moving along perfectly.

The next day Jean had coffee, fried herself an egg for breakfast, then went downstairs to tidy up. She had three coffins, nice ones, but no one in Apple Blossom could afford them except maybe the Featherstones or the Watsons. She had some lumber behind the funeral parlor for simple pine boxes. Maybe Wallis could help her make a couple. One never knew when they'd need them, just as no one expected her to need so many the day the posse rode out after those wretched outlaws.

She took a quick inventory, jotted everything down, then made a list. That done, she thought she'd drop by the hotel and tell Dora about the library.

As soon as she walked in the kitchen, Dora gasped. "There you are – at last! Sit, have some coffee, then tell me everything." She hurried to the stove and brought the pot to the table.

Jean noticed there was an extra cup and saucer, and watched Dora fill it. "You were expecting me?"

"Always am." Dora returned the pot to the stove. "So? The library?"

She smacked the table. "Wallis told you? I wanted it to be a surprise."

Dora's hands went to her hips. "Did you specifically tell him not to say anything?"

Jean's face fell. "No."

"Well, there you have it. Next time make him swear."

Jean picked up her cup. "I didn't think he'd tell anyone. For him it's not that exciting."

"How do you know?" Dora sat across from her. "Maybe he's happy for you and that's why he shared."

Jean glanced her way, then spooned some sugar into her cup. "He went with me to speak to Mr. Featherstone."

Dora grinned. "See, he took the trouble to help you."

Jean gave her cup a stir. "The Darlings have been taking the trouble to help everyone. Even me."

Dora frowned. "Don't talk like that. I know you need the help, don't pretend you don't."

She eyed the cream. "It was embarrassing letting him see my place yesterday. Especially after we looked at the library."

"You have nothing to be ashamed of."

Jean tried not to gape at her. "Easy for you to say – you have this beautiful hotel. One Phileas will make even better once he gets to it."

Dora rolled her eyes. "If he gets to it. He interrogated poor Wallis last night over dinner as if he worked for the sheriff."

Jean's breath hitched. Wallis must have said something. Did his brothers think they were courting now? Oh, heavens. What should she say?

Dora smiled. "So, you and Wallis spent a lot of time together yesterday afternoon?"

"Not that long. Not after the news Irving gave everyone. I wonder how Sarah's feeling?"

"I would think it would be obvious," Dora said as she set down her cup. "She's in love, Jean. I'm happy for her, aren't you?"

A pang of guilt hit, and she tried to ignore it. Unfortunately, it crept into her cheeks as a blush.

Dora smiled. "What is it?"

She caught the teasing tone in Dora's voice and tried not to grimace. "Nothing. I haven't said a word." Dora's eyes narrowed in suspicion. Jean had to think fast. "Did he tell you about Agnes?"

Doris sat back and rolled her eyes. "For once I'd like her to keep her nose out of everybody's business."

Jean frowned. "Seeing as they gave the biggest donation to the library to see it built, I don't think that's going to happen. Agnes will consider everything I do as volunteer work."

"If a lot of people volunteered, yes. But you should be compensated if you're the only one taking care of the place." Dora went to the stove and opened the warming oven. She took out a covered bowl and brought it to the table. "Here, have a muffin. You look like you need one."

She took it and set it on the table. "Butter?"

Dora brought a crock from the hutch and placed it before her. "What did Wallis say about your place?"

"That it was ridiculously small." She took a bite of blueberry muffin. It was delicious.

"He said nothing of the kind."

Jean smiled. She knew her well. "He said little. Other than he'd come back to inspect it for repairs." She took another bite and tried to think of a way to change the subject.

"So ... he told his brothers that ..." Dora looked gleeful. "... he thought you were pretty."

Jean stopped chewing. Wallis *did* say something to get them thinking. The question was, should she play along? Once she started, she was in. But it was only for a few days, so ... "Well, I do think he's sort of handsome."

Dora laughed. "I knew it!"

Jean jumped. "Knew what? That I thought he was attractive?"

"No, that there was something between you two." Dora grabbed a muffin and slathered it with butter.

Jean stared at her in shock. "But there's nothing ... I mean ..."

Dora took a bite. "You can deny it all you want," she said and chewed. As soon as she swallowed, she grinned again. "But I could tell there was something."

Jean stared at her own muffin. "I don't know about that ..."

"Question is ..." Dora took another bite.

Jean had to wait for her to finish chewing and then swallow. Just what *did* Wallis tell everyone?

"... are the two of you getting sweet on each other?"

Jean gasped.

"Don't look so shocked." Dora put more butter on her muffin. "I've seen him steal glances at you."

Her jaw dropped. "You have? When?"

"You're here almost every night for dinner."

She thought a moment. She was right. And though she'd never paid much attention to Wallis, maybe he was paying her more notice than she'd realized. "Oh, dear."

Dora smiled and chewed. She devoured her muffin, a clear sign she was excited. It wasn't because of Wallis, was it? "He said nothing last night about being sweet on me?" She cringed waiting for the answer.

"Not in so many words," Dora said with another grin. "But he admitted he thought you were attractive."

Jean gave her a stern look. "And you heard him say this."

Dora closed one eye and shrugged. "Well, not exactly. Conrad told me."

Jean buried her face in her hands. "Oh, good grief." She let her hands drop. "I suppose that doesn't surprise me." She looked at the table for a moment, then Dora. "Did he say anything else?"

"You are a little sweet on him, aren't you?" Dora prodded.

Jean groaned. "He's going to help me with the library and my place. Whether we ..." Uh-oh, she didn't want to go too far in the other direction. "Well, should something spark between us, I'm sure everyone will know."

Dora smiled with an exaggerated wink. "More coffee?"

Jean sighed and pushed the cup and saucer toward her. Dora took it to the stove and refilled it. "Where are they?" she asked.

"The Darlings? At Sarah's place. They're tearing out the floor. Sarah, Flint and Lacey went with them."

"Oh, yes. I'd quite forgotten." She sipped her coffee, finished her muffin, then took her cup and saucer to the sink. "I'd better get going. I need to speak with Mr. Atkins."

"Is he coming to town today?"

"I'm not sure. But I'll find out." That meant asking Alma. Mr. Atkins usually told her when he was bringing lumber to town.

"If not, are you going to walk to the Atkins' place or drive out?" Dora asked.

"I could do with a little exercise, but I might still saddle my horse and ride out." Besides, it meant she'd have to walk by Sarah's house. With a little luck, she could speak with Wallis about what he told everyone last night. She didn't like being left in the dark.

"Suit yourself." Dora put the muffins back in the warming oven, gave her a hug, then put her own cup and saucer in the sink.

She'd seen her do these simple tasks hundreds of times, yet there was a bounce in Dora's step that hadn't been there before. Merciful heavens, was she already sweet on Phileas? Or maybe one of the others? What if it was Wallis? "I'll see you later, Dora."

She waved, grabbed the kettle off the stove and headed for the back door.

Jean watched her go, eyes narrowed in suspicion. If Dora was sweet on Phileas, had he reciprocated? If so, then Wallis' plan was moot. There was no sense in pretending to court if love had already struck the other pair. She left the hotel and headed for the general store, surprised at the disappointment settling in her belly. It would have been nice to have Wallis pay attention to her for a few days, even if he was pretending.

When she reached the store, she sighed and went inside. If Alma had heard about their "courting," it would be too much. She'd spread it all over town and by the end of the day have them married.

Darn if Jean didn't smile at the thought, though.

Chapter Five

Wallis tied a kerchief around his neck and pulled it over his nose and mouth. They were tearing out the floors in Sarah Crawford's bedroom today and he was doing his best to endure the stench. It lingered everywhere. "Skunks. I'm so glad we don't have them in England."

"I wholeheartedly agree," Irving said. "Good gracious, what a smell!"

Sterling pulled another nail from a floorboard. "The sooner we get it done the better, chaps."

Wallis tackled another corner of the room. Having a family of skunks living under the house wasn't pleasant. How did Sarah and her children stand the smell? The reek carried through the house, permeating the walls. Walls no doubt bathed in the musty smell of a family that lived in fear of their own home. And he'd suggested to Jean she buy the place. What was he thinking?

He continued to work and concluded he was overreacting, but after seeing Jean's tiny hovel, he wanted her to have a bigger home. This would be perfect once they fixed it up. The new interior paint looked good, and with the new bedroom floor and other repairs – and the skunks gone – she'd have a fine little house.

To be honest, he didn't know how Sarah and her kids put up with living with the stench. He felt a wave of pity for them and thought they should do something to keep the skunks from returning. He'd find a way, especially if Jean could buy or rent the place. A few strategic repairs could get rid of any lingering odors, and the house was an excellent opportunity for Jean to move into a home with plenty of room.

They worked another hour, then took a break. Wallis pulled the kerchief down and breathed in some fresh air. The smell wouldn't have been so bad if Oliver hadn't scared the creatures when he inspected the floorboards. But it had to be done. Now poor Ollie was doing his best to avoid everyone, poor chap.

Conrad wiped the back of his neck with his kerchief. "Hey, isn't that Jean?"

Wallis looked toward the road. Sure enough, he spied her riding Mr. Brown, her gray gelding. He smiled at the horse's name and wiped the sweat from his brow. "I wonder where she's off to?"

"Is she coming here?" Sterling asked.

Wallis didn't answer and watched her stop at the new picket fence. She wore a wide-brimmed hat, a blue dress and an apron. She must have forgotten to take it off before she left. The fact she was riding astride reminded him where he was. One would never see an English-woman in anything but a sidesaddle.

He headed her way. "Hello there."

She smiled, dismounted, and tied Mr. Brown's reins to the fence. "How's the work coming along?"

"Good. We're taking a break." He looked the horse over. He was a sturdy creature, his coat a pale gray brushed with silver. In the sunlight, the mane and tail shimmered like moonlight rippling on a pond. The gelding was also part of her work. When she had work, that is.

Jean smiled as she looked at the picket fence and front yard. "This is lovely."

He laughed. "It's new. And the yard's cleaned up a bit. There's fresh paint inside, but I'm not sure you want to go in there."

She scrunched up her face. "The smell?"

He nodded. "It's still bad."

"It will get better with time. Poor Sarah." She looked around. "Where is she?"

"She and the children walked to Letty's for lunch."

Jean continued to study the house. "How does she feel about all this?"

"The house?"

She half-smiled. "Leaving it, I mean. I always thought

this to be a cute little place." She turned around and gazed down the road. "It's close to town, yet private."

"That it is." He joined her at the fence. "You could live here, you know. We could speak to Irving and Sarah about it."

She glanced his way as she blushed. "I can't, Wallis."

"With a little help, you could."

She faced the road. "Nothing is for certain. Not even a position at the library. I was excited before, but now I'm being realistic."

Wallis ran a hand over the top of the fence. He knew her situation, and therefore her fear. But what could he do about it? Yesterday she was so happy to take over the library. But now he saw doubt etched in her features. He frowned. She had to find the courage to stick to her plan.

Hmm, maybe he could help. For starters, he could reassure her she was capable, and would run the library. She had to believe in herself and her capabilities. Now all he had to do was inspire her confidence.

He exhaled and stepped closer to the fence. "Listen, you don't have to do this if you're not ready. There's no shame in that. I'm sure you have plenty of skills and knowledge, but if you're not ready, then you must take charge of that. Don't let fear dictate your decisions and stop you from doing something great."

She gaped at him a moment, then took off her hat. "I know I'm being a coward. But after thinking about everything, the library is enough to start with. I don't have to have a new place to live. And there are no guarantees. Even if Sarah wanted to rent me this house, the library won't be enough to cover it monthly."

He steeled himself and looked her in the eyes. "Look, I know things are difficult for you right now, but you can do this. I also know it's scary, but the library is something special, and you can make it even better. You just need to have faith in yourself." He reached over the fence and took her hands, squeezing them tightly. "No matter what happens, I'm here for you. We can do this together, okay?"

To his surprise, she looked into his eyes, the fear in her own slowly melting away. "Okay," she said, nodding.

Wallis smiled in relief. "You won't regret it, Jean. I know it'll be work, but you'll have help."

She laughed and pulled her hands from his. "Thank you. But how are we going to do all of this in the short time you're still here?"

He swallowed. It was a good question. He glanced down the road. He couldn't think about it right now. "What are you doing out here, anyway?"

"I was on my way to speak to Mr. Atkins about getting supplies to build more shelves."

He smiled. "Good." He reached into the inside pocket of his vest and pulled out a small pad. "Give him these." He tore off the sheet of paper with the shelf measurements he'd jotted down yesterday.

She took it and put it in her apron pocket. "Thank you." She looked past him and waved.

Wallis turned around as Sterling approached. "I

should get back to work. Give Mr. Atkins the measurements and tell him I'll take care of the cost."

"But Wallis ..."

"Don't argue – someone has to. You don't have any donation money to work with."

Her eyes widened. "Oh, dear, you're right. What was I thinking?"

"Excitement will do that to you. Are you excited again?" He hoped she said yes.

She nodded. "Thank you for supporting me in this, Wallis. I appreciate it."

Sterling joined them with a smile. "Hello, Jean. What brings you out here?"

"She was just heading to Woodrow's for some lumber. We're building library shelves."

Sterling folded his arms. "Is that so? Good for you. The town could use the library." He winked at Wallis and strolled away.

Jean watched Sterling a moment then arched an eyebrow at Wallis. "What was that about? You said something to your brothers last night, didn't you?"

He tried to look innocent. "About what?"

"Don't play dumb. You said something about our courting each other."

He gave her a sheepish shrug. "I might have mentioned that ... I thought ..."

"... that you found me attractive?" she finished.

Whoops, caught! But he did think she was pretty. "Let them think what they want," he finally said. He

64

forced himself to turn away. She looked prettier today than yesterday. She'd piled her thick brown hair on top of her head, some of which had loosened and curled around her neck. Her brown eyes were as warm and inviting as they'd ever been, and her skin glowed with health. Though dressed in a plain dress and apron, it only added to her beauty.

He even caught the little blush on her cheeks as she looked at the fence, a shy smile on her face. It took all his strength to break his gaze and turn away. Maybe spending a lot of time with her while working on the library wasn't such a good idea. "I need to go."

"All right." She smiled in parting and untied Mr. Brown's reins. Once mounted she looked over her shoulder and waved. "I'll see you later, Wallis."

He returned the wave and watched as she rode away. All she needed was a little encouragement, and he admired how it brought out her strength and independence. Now he had to make sure she hung onto it. She'd need it for what she was trying to accomplish.

When he could no longer see her, Wallis ran a hand over the fence and smiled. No matter what happened, he'd make sure she had the courage and strength to be successful in this. He wanted nothing more than to see her succeed. He just hoped and prayed he didn't fall in love with her in the process.

"I've got some extra pieces here I can donate," Mr. Atkins said. "Follow me."

"Thank you." Jean trailed after him as he led her into a shed full of different sized pieces of lumber.

"See that stack?" He pointed to some long rectangular planks. "Think they'd be wide enough?"

Jean examined them. "They're perfect."

"That's pine. It's a softer wood, mind, but will do for shelving."

"I can ride back to town and return with my wagon."

"No need. I'm heading into town tomorrow to fetch a few supplies for myself. I can bring them along."

She took out Wallis' measurements. "Can you cut them for me?" She handed him the paper.

Mr. Atkins looked it over. "Sure, no problem. What else are you looking for?"

"That's it for now. Mr. Darling – that is, Wallis – will help me fix my place up but I don't think he'll need much for that."

Mr. Atkins grinned as he scratched the back of his neck. "Jean, I don't mind telling you that wreck of a building should be torn down."

She cringed. "But Mr. Atkins, it's all I have."

"It's old."

She sighed. It was true. When her family moved to Apple Blossom, she was young; the funeral parlor, not so much. It was probably one of the first buildings in town. Sure, it needed a paint job and some repairs, but it was still structurally sound. Wasn't it? "I can work with it."

"I know, child," he said. "But I don't think it will last much longer. You need a stronger foundation and I'm afraid that one ain't gonna cut it."

"But I don't have the money. I'm not even sure where I'd get it."

Jean met the older man's gaze as he smiled. "Well, if you've got one of them Darlings offering to help, then you'd best take advantage." Mr. Atkins shuffled back into the shed.

Her stomach churned and her heart raced as she followed him. "The building is all I have." Egad, was that desperation in her voice?

Mr. Atkins shook his head as he stopped, then turned to face her. "No, I don't mean you have to tear it down. Not yet anyway. I'm merely suggesting you give it a little love and care. And I'm here to help," he finished, smiling. "I'm willing to donate a few things."

Jean felt her heart warm. It wasn't every day that someone offered help expecting nothing in return. Except maybe the Darlings. But then, so far, they were getting plenty in return: Letty, Cassie and now Sarah. Would she be next? She doubted it. "Thank you," she said, voice thick with emotion.

He smiled again. "You're welcome. Now, let's see what else I have around here that you can use."

They left the shed and went into a large barn containing multiple stacks of lumber, each a different size. "I don't know what I'll need here," she said. "Wallis hasn't inspected my place yet."

"But he's seen it?"

"Oh, yes. Yesterday, in fact. But we were more concerned with the library. The sooner I can get it up and running, the sooner I can tend to my place."

"You're going to need donations for the library, ain't ya? The missus and I have a few books we can give. And the lumber for the shelves, of course." He smiled and led her to the back of the barn. "I've got some small pieces here that would work with the shelves. I'll dig them out."

"Thank you, Mr. Atkins. I don't know what to say." While he had his back turned, she quickly wiped her eyes. She wasn't expecting him to donate anything.

"It's no problem. Besides, it'll be nice to know these get put to use." He held up a wooden scrolled bracket. "Just have Wallis use these. I can give you what I have, and if you need more, I'll make some."

She closed her eyes a moment. Everything Wallis told her over the fence not only made her feel better, but stronger, more confident. And now this. Maybe she could rent Sarah's house. But she would still need another source of income. "I'll let him know. Thank you so much, Mr. Atkins. What can I do to repay you?"

"No need, Jean. This town has had a rough time of it. We still need to pull together, take care of each other. Besides, I like to read."

She smiled, her eyes misting, and wiped them again. First Wallis and now this. Both were right. She had to forge ahead, get the work done, live her life. Not that Mr. Atkins said that in so many words, but without the funeral parlor and now the library, what did she have? Absolutely nothing.

"I'll gather everything together and bring it to town tomorrow. Can you meet me at the library?"

"What time?" Her heart pounded. She was getting excited to start. A far cry from when she'd saddled Mr. Brown earlier and left town.

The more she thought about her conversation with Dora that morning, though, the more her heart sank. All her friends were finding love except her. And they all had something to offer a future husband. Letty had her ranch, Cassie was the sheriff and gave Conrad a job as deputy. Sarah topped both by giving Irving a family.

And what did she have to offer? A few coffins and a ramshackle funeral parlor with two small rooms over it to live in. Who in their right mind would want any part of that? But if she had the library, and one other job, there was hope. Maybe some handsome strangers would come to town again one day.

Mr. Atkins prepared a list of everything he was donating, gave it to her, then sent her on her way. She couldn't wait to tell Wallis and stopped at Sarah's on the way back to town.

After she tied Mr. Brown to the fence, she went around to the back of the house. There was a lot of grunting, the sound of wood being tossed onto a pile, and the overpowering smell of skunk spray. She waved her hand in front of her face. "Oh, goodness." She pulled a handkerchief out of her sleeve and put it over her nose and mouth.

"Jean," Irving said when he saw her. "What brings you here? I heard you came by earlier."

"Where's Wallis? I need to tell him something."

"He's inside. Be careful – don't go into Sarah's bedroom. Over half the floor is torn out."

She nodded and entered through the back door. The rest of the Darlings were in the bedroom pulling up floorboards. "Wallis?"

He poked his head around the corner of the door. "Jean." He put both hands on either side of the door-jamb and stepped up into the kitchen. "Join me in the parlor. It's not as noisy in there."

She followed him into the other room and stood by the front door. "You won't believe what just happened. Mr. Atkins is donating all the lumber for the shelves."

Wallis wiped sweat from his brow with a red kerchief. "That's wonderful!" He sat down on the worn sofa.

She joined him, her excitement growing. "He even gave us some scrolled wooden brackets to support them and said he'd make more if needed."

Wallis beamed. "Jolly good."

Jean smiled as she realized she was no longer alone in her struggles. Yes, she had Letty and Dora, but this was different. She now had the right people by her side. Most of all, she had Wallis. Together they could make this work.

He leaned in, a radiant smile on his face. "Now we

need the town's support. I'm sure once they find out about the library, the donations will start pouring in."

Jean nodded as her chest warmed. In a short time, he made her feel alive again and given her a purpose. Now she was ready to make her dreams come true. Part of them, anyway. But what she really wanted wasn't in reach. Not yet. Unfortunately, by the time it was, Wallis would be gone. She swallowed hard then put on a smile. "I'm ready to get to work."

He smiled back, his eyes never leaving her face. "Then let's get started. Your library is going to be beautiful."

Jean caught the pride in his eyes and felt like her heart would burst. How did he do this, make her feel like she could take on the world? But he was right – if she was ever going to succeed, she knew she had to start now. And having Wallis by her side was the best thing that had ever happened to her. "I don't know how I can ever repay you for all your help."

Wallis grinned and shook his head. "No repayment necessary. I want to help." He stood and offered his arm.

She gratefully accepted. "Thank you. I'll be forever in your debt."

He gave her hand a tender pat. "It's my pleasure."

They smiled at each other, and Jean's heart skipped a beat. She'd always remember this moment, and not just because of the library or the fact Wallis gave her such confidence.

As they walked into the kitchen, the hole left behind by her father's passing wasn't so big anymore.

Chapter Six

When they finished tearing out the floor, Wallis and his brothers cleaned up the stray pieces of old flooring, nails and whatnot, and tossed them into the refuse pile. They could either use the old boards for firewood and hope the smell of skunk dissipated quickly as it burned or store it for winter and hope by then the stench would have left it.

Wallis smiled to himself as he thought of poor Oliver. He still couldn't join them because of the stench clinging to him. It was just as bad today as yesterday.

Wallis smiled again. He and his brothers decided they would call the floor "Oliver's Floor." It was a small joke to ease the discomfort, but it went a long way to making everybody feel better. Once the new floor was in and the room painted, it would be brighter and more inviting. But no matter what it looked like, Wallis knew the room had its own special charm thanks to Oliver. Because of him, they had a story they could all laugh at, and a reminder that no matter how bad things seemed, in time they can turn out okay.

When they returned to town, his brothers went straight to the hotel to clean up, but Wallis went to Jean's. He needed to give the place a full inspection, write everything he thought it might need, then speak to Mr. Atkins when he brought the lumber to the library tomorrow. As soon as that was done, he'd join his brothers at Sarah's house and get to work.

He tried the door at the funeral parlor. It was unlocked, so he went inside. The room was not only small, but he noticed things he'd missed yesterday. The wallpaper was peeling, the furniture worn, and the hardwood floors scratched and stained. He frowned, knowing Jean had her hands full with this place. She'd work herself to the bone to make things better if she had to work alone.

He inspected the room, noting every detail, and tried to come up with a plan for the renovation, how to move things around, where furniture would go and what materials he would need for repairs. Now that he'd had a gander, he looked forward to the challenge. He wanted the first floor of the tiny building to reflect the personality of its proprietor, even if it was a funeral parlor.

He went outside and around to the back to see the building from a different angle, taking in the complete picture. After putting all the pieces of what needed to be done together in his head, he smiled, already envisioning how it would look when he was done. If he could do everything he wanted, it would make Jean proud.

He'd create a space of love and rest instead of one of despair and gloom. This wouldn't be a building of darkness, but one adorned with light and compassion where those mourning could find solace. With the completion of the renovation, Wallis was sure Jean would look at it differently too. She'd lost her mother, her father, and the rest of the posse ...

"Wallis," she said as she came out the back door. "What are you doing here?"

"Looking at the place." He jotted a few more things down. "The building needs to be painted."

"Yes. I know." She joined him and studied it. "As you can see, the original paint has worn off. Now that you're getting a good look, what do you think?"

He mustered up a smile. "We'll get as much done as we can before I leave. I'm sure Mr. Atkins and the captain will help after that."

She nodded. "It's going to be a lot of work."

He gave her the same look of encouragement he had during their talk at the fence. "You'll get it done. We'll make this a cheery place."

"Cheery?" She laughed. "Wallis, it's a funeral parlor. There's nothing cheery about it."

"Comforting, then." He noted a few more things, then returned the pad and pencil to his pocket.

"Did you look at all of it?"

"Only the first floor – everything but the storeroom." He headed for the back door. He hadn't noticed it before. When he entered the building, he went to the storeroom and stepped inside. His primary concern was the floor. Now that he had a good idea of how much work was involved in tearing one out, he'd want that work done while he and his brothers were still in town.

He walked over to the corner where Jean said she used to sleep and knelt to inspect some scratch marks on the floor. He could just imagine Jean sleeping on some rickety cot with a moth-eaten blanket to keep her warm. He ran his fingers over the floor and realized she'd slept here for years. After all, it hadn't been long since she lost her father.

She joined him. "What did you find?"

He got to his feet. "Nothing, just checking the boards." He turned around to find her leaning against the doorjamb. "It doesn't look too bad in here. But you have some bad floorboards in the main room."

She looked sheepish. "I know. Pa meant to fix them but never got around to it. When he came home from working with Mr. Atkins or Mr. Smythe, he was plumb tuckered out."

"Understandable. I'm rather tuckered out myself." He smiled. "Now, how about we look upstairs?"

She began to fidget. "Didn't you get a good look last time?"

He noticed her blush and realized she was embarrassed. "It's like I said earlier, we need to get as much done as we can while I'm here. If I must enlist the help of my brothers, I will."

She crossed her arms and smiled. "You mean Phileas?"

He smiled back. "He would be the obvious choice."

She entered the room. "I don't think you have to worry about the two of us pretending to court. Considering all this work, we'll be spending a lot of time together. People can draw their own conclusions."

"True, and if Phileas is helping us, all the better."

"But when it comes time for you to leave, what if he wants to stay to work on the hotel? If you take up all his time, would he do that?"

Wallis blanched. It was a good question. He'd asked it himself recently, then promptly brushed it aside. Phileas, already determined to work on the hotel, could indeed stay behind to fulfill his artistic mission. Egad, how horrible would that be? He might never come back to England. "He could," he said with a gulp.

Jean went to the corner where she used to sleep and stared at the floor. "Would that be so bad?"

Wallis, his hand to his chest, turned to her. "Phileas staying?"

She nodded.

Oh, dear. Jean, along with the rest of the town, didn't know who he and his brothers really were. Future family members excluded, of course. Letty, Cassie, and Sarah hadn't said a word to anyone, and for that he and his brothers were grateful. "I suppose it would depend on *why* he stayed. So long as he came home after working on the hotel our mother wouldn't fall apart. But if he stayed because of love …"

Her head came up. "So what if he did? Doesn't your mother want him to be happy?"

He opened and closed his mouth a few times, but the words wouldn't come. He cleared his throat and had another go. "In time I would hope so."

"And your father?"

He rolled his eyes. "That's a good question." He would not tell her that the only thing Father cared about was the Darlington name being carried on, along with the title and the estate. Father never dreamed his sons would find love in America and not return. Neither did he or his brothers.

"Wallis?"

He snapped to attention. "Let's go upstairs, shall we?" He headed for the door.

She followed him up to her living quarters. Like downstairs, her tiny parlor/kitchen needed repairs. As he looked around, Wallis noted what materials they'd need: wood, nails, paint, fabric.

"So what do you think?"

He turned to her, noting the worry in her eyes, then pulled out his notepad so he could make a list. "We'll start with the walls, then move onto the fixtures and furniture." He forced a smile, his mind still on Phileas. "It'll be fun. We'll have this place looking tip-top again in no time at all."

"Fun?" Jean smiled. "We'll be working hard."

"But it's work we can enjoy. And I'm sure by the end, this building will be as beautiful as it was before. The captain and Woodrow can do some of the heavy lifting, but right now, we should get started since I'll be gone soon. Between this and the library, we have a lot to do."

She nodded, biting her lower lip. "I never mentioned my budget. I don't think we can get it done with what I have."

Wallis hated to see uncertainty in her eyes, and right now, they were full of it. He took her hands. "Did I not tell you earlier you can do this?"

"You did, but we were talking about the library. And Mr. Atkins donated all the wood for the shelves. I doubt he'll donate much for this place."

Wallis looked her in the eyes and hoped this wasn't a mistake. "Perhaps not. But I'm willing to."

Jean watched Wallis scribble as he inspected her bedroom. She knew her place was clean yet shabby, a combination that couldn't be helped with Pa's meager savings. Peeling wallpaper, creaky floorboards, and broken drawers were familiar sights to her. She felt nervous and wondered what Wallis thought now that he was getting a good look around. Her eyes flicked to the drafty windows. His scrutiny didn't surprise her. Drafts were a less than satisfactory experience for any guest.

"I can work with what you have here," he said. "We could put up new wallpaper and get you a decent bed frame. Maybe even put some rugs on the floor to brighten up the place." He continued writing things down before adding, "This space may take a lot of work, but I'm sure with the right ideas, it could look great."

Jean smiled. She never thought about adding a few items to make the place look good. Her family's two rooms were just that, rooms. They served a purpose and there was no call for fripperies. "Those are great ideas. I'm not sure about new wallpaper, though."

Wallis smiled. "Why not speak to Alma? Maybe she has some she can sell at a discount. I can take care of that too."

Her hand flew to her chest as it tightened. "No one's ever done so much for me. I ... don't know what to say, Wallis."

He stuffed his pad and pencil in a pocket and looked her in the eyes. "Jean, we're here to help, remember? You don't have to say anything. Now, I'll get started on gathering the supplies we'll need. I'm sure we can transform this room into something you'll love, not to mention a nice quiet place to read."

Her other hand went to her chest as she fought against tears. She didn't know why she was so emotional. Maybe because she wasn't expecting him to work on her place to the extent he wanted to. If she couldn't afford Sarah's house, then these two rooms were all she had.

Why not make them nice? "Thank you." Her lower lip trembled, and she bit it.

"There, there," he consoled. "Everything will look wonderful when we're done. The library included."

A tiny laugh escaped. "Thank you."

He continued to look into her eyes, and she found she couldn't look away. Wallis, like the rest of his brothers, had beautiful blue eyes. Wallis' were different though. There was a kindness in them that warmed her from the inside. She smiled back without thinking.

He sidled toward the door and broke the strange connection. "Right. We have a lot of work to do. I'm sure you have a list of things you'd like to have done. Let me know what I can do to help."

Jean nodded, still unable to think. He was right, there was a lot to do. She wanted her home to look nice again and was now willing to put in the work to do it. The place hadn't looked decent since before her mother died. Taking a deep breath, she tried to picture the room with new wallpaper and curtains as he had.

"I should get going," he said, breaking into her thoughts. "I'll see you soon."

Jean blinked, realizing she was still staring at him. "Yes, see you soon."

She watched Wallis leave and looked at her bedroom. This project was going to be the start of something special. Maybe after everything was done, she wouldn't feel like she was some dark cloud hanging over Apple Blossom. After all, she'd buried everyone's loved ones after the incident. It wasn't something she'd soon forget and wondered if she'd have the same nightmares if she had to bury anyone else.

She didn't want to think about it, so went into the kitchen to make some tea, and realized she was out. Part of her wanted to go to the hotel and have a cup with Dora. If she did, she might see Wallis again and maybe they could exchange more ideas about the library and her little home. It would also give people reason to believe they were sweet on each other. But was it necessary?

She took some money from a tin box in her bedroom, then headed out the door.

Alma was dusting shelves behind the counter when Jean arrived at the general store. As soon as the bell over the door rang, she turned around. "Jean!"

Uh-oh. She took a step back. Someone must have said something to her.

Alma hurried around the counter, feather duster in hand and stood before her with a happy smile. "How romantic!"

Her eyebrows shot up. "What?"

"You and Mr. Darling. Which one is it again, Wallis or Phileas?"

Yep. Someone said something. "Wallis. He's helping me with the library and my place."

"What better way to show his affection?" Alma gushed.

Jean glanced around the store. Who could have told her? *What* did they tell her? "He's just helping out."

"Sure he is." Alma winked.

Jean tried to ignore the comment and went to the counter. "I'm out of tea."

Alma trotted behind it, grabbed a few jars off the shelves, and placed them before her. "Which one?"

"What's this?" She picked up a jar to examine it. "Loose-leaf tea? But you've never carried this in the store before. You've only sold bricks."

"I know, but I splurged and ordered some of this because of the Darlings. Sterling and Phileas have both said they would die without a proper cup of tea."

Jean sighed as she ran her finger across the counter. "I had no idea. I suspect they're eager to get back to England."

"Not Sterling and Conrad."

Jean tried not grimace. "We don't know that. They could decide to marry and go home."

"What?" Alma said with wide eyes. "But Letty and Cassie can't leave Apple Blossom. What would we do without them?"

"Go on." There, she said it. She'd have to go on with her life without them just like everyone else. One more reason to get the library up and running. It would be something to fill her days.

"You look sad," Alma pointed out.

She tried not to roll her eyes. Of course she looked sad. She might have to say goodbye to her friends. "I'm fine."

Alma shrugged then tapped each jar with a finger. "Rose, white, and Earl Grey."

Jean studied the three jars. "Let me try the rose."

Alma produced a small bag and began spooning tea into it. "Are you excited about Letty's wedding?"

Her heart sank. How could she feel so good while in Wallis' company, and as soon as he was gone, so terrible? "When is it?"

"I thought you would know."

"I don't."

"Guaranteed it will be before the Darlings leave. Unless Rev. Arnold leaves first. Then he'll have to do something right away."

She nodded. "Maybe he'll perform a triple wedding." Good grief, she hoped not. Then the Darlings would be gone, just like that. How long did she have, then? A week? Ten days? Either way, Wallis wasn't staying.

Alma slid the bag of tea across the counter. "You're being awful quiet."

She shrugged. "I have a lot on my mind."

"I should say so, what with the library and all. And they're going to work on your place too?"

Jean smiled. "Wallis had some good ideas on how to decorate it. I have to admit, I was surprised."

Alma beamed. "Like I said, romantic." She came around the counter. "Do you think you'll fall in love?"

Jean gasped. "What kind of question is that? Besides, I doubt Wallis has any interest in me."

Alma's jaw dropped. "Why not? You're pretty, smart, kind ..."

"... and the undertaker."

Alma's face screwed up. "Oh. There is that." She clasped her hands in front of her and hurried back behind the counter.

Jean paid her, took her bag of tea, then went to the small table of books. There was nothing new. "Where do you order your books from?" She had a good guess but might as well ask.

"The catalogue, of course." Alma joined her. "Once you open the library, I might as well not sell them anymore. But that's okay, it gives me space for something else."

"Could I order from the catalogue?"

She shrugged. "I don't see why not. Since it's for a library, you might get a discount. You should write the catalogue people and find out."

"I can do that?" She frowned. Obviously, she had a few things to learn.

"Yes, and if other libraries want to get rid of some of their inventory, let them know you're interested. I would start with the library in Bozeman. Theirs is much bigger than Virginia City's."

"Thanks, Alma. This helps a lot."

She smiled. "Did you need anything else?"

Jean's eyes gravitated to the rack of ready-made clothes. What she wouldn't give for a new dress. She headed for them. It wouldn't hurt to look. She pulled a brown day dress trimmed in white lace off the rack. It sported a wide, brown satin sash at the waist.

"That is lovely," Alma commented. "If brown is too plain for you, I have some blue and pink ones as well."

"The brown isn't too plain." She ran a hand across the soft material and sighed.

Alma reached for a nearby box. "Here's the matching hat." She pulled it out. It had a brown satin band and had a feather in it. "See? It's pretty."

Yes, it was. But she knew she couldn't buy it. As much as she longed for some new clothes, it wasn't in her budget right now. What clothes she had were serviceable and would have to do. "It is nice. But I think I'll wait until I'm finished with the library and my house."

Alma smiled and put the hat back in the box.

Jean returned the dress to the rack. "I think it's time I went home."

"Of course," Alma said. "And don't worry about the Darlings. They'll figure out what to do."

"I hope so." Jean left the store, feeling a little better about things. Sure, the Darlings were leaving and that would be hard. But at least she was making progress on her own dreams. She could only hope those dreams came true and she wouldn't regret taking this step.

Chapter Seven

Wallis went to the hotel, changed his clothes and went downstairs. It was too early for dinner and he wondered if Jean would join them. No matter, he could always stop by her place and invite her. In the meantime, he'd wander across the street to Alma's store and see what she had in the way of fabric for curtains.

As he stepped out of the hotel, the air was warm, and he realized it had been too long since he'd gone for a quiet walk and enjoyed the fresh air. He took a deep breath and started across the street. Maybe Jean would like to take a walk with him.

When he entered the store, he smiled at the sound of the bell over the door and took in the colorful displays of goods. There were shelves filled with bolts of fabrics of all colors, patterns, and textures. He took a few moments to peruse the selections and found the perfect fabric for

Jean's bedroom curtains, but she'd have the final say. She might hate his pick.

He continued to look around, surprised Alma hadn't seen him. No matter, he could do with a minute of peace. He surveyed the canned goods, tools and various sundries. More fabrics of various kinds were stacked on the far end of the counter and along the wall. There were skeins of yarn and small folded pieces of colorful cloth, probably for quilting. He also spotted jars of buttons, reels of ribbon, and spools of lace. He ran his hand across some bolts of fabric and wondered if Jean would like any of them for a new dress.

Alma stepped out of the back storeroom carrying a bolt of white fabric. "Hello," she said, "Jean was in here recently."

Wallis couldn't hide his surprise. "Was she?"

Alma smiled. "She was out of tea. What can I do for you?"

He shrugged. "I'm here to pick out fabric for curtains. Maybe a rug or two."

She nodded. "For the library?" A blush crept into her cheeks. "Or Jean's place?"

He smiled. One had to be careful when speaking with Alma. She was excitable, and who knew what she'd tell other folks when they came into the store? "Both."

"Fine. Look at these." She headed for the shelf containing bolts of fabric. She had him sort through the selections, and, after choosing two colors and a variety of textures, started discussing rug options. Wallis was glad Jean wasn't there. He wanted to surprise her with what he picked. He was no Phileas, but he had good taste.

By the time they finished he had a small stack of fabric, several small rugs, and a few bags of tea on the counter. "Did Jean mention if she needed anything else while she was here?"

Alma glanced at something across the store. "She had her eye on a dress." She grinned and was off like a shot. "It's over here."

Wallis smiled at her enthusiasm. Alma either covered her grief well or was the sort of person who was always happy.

She pulled a brown calico dress off the rack. "This one."

He studied it. "Would it fit her?"

Alma held it against herself. "I think so. We're about the same size." She grinned again. "Are you going to get it for her?"

He studied the dress then glanced at the others on the rack. "This one is nice, but ..."

Alma smiled, took a pink day dress from the rack and held it up. "I think this would look lovely on Jean."

Wallis looked the dress over. It had a soft flowing skirt, a delicate print of rosebuds and an embroidered collar. "That's perfect. Yes, I think Jean should have that one." He blinked a few times. Great Scott, what was he saying?!

"She might also like this one." Alma pulled another

off the rack. The blue dress had long sleeves and a sweet-heart neckline with a stiffened ruffled skirt.

"I don't know …" He also didn't know why he was considering dresses for Jean. It's not as if they were … oh. So *that's* what was going on.

"This is very nice," Alma said. "I think Jean would look lovely in it too." She smiled brightly. "Unless you prefer this one." She returned the dress to the rack and pulled off another. This one was purple with a lace collar, a short bodice with a bell skirt and a white bow in the back. "This would be perfect for her. It's simple, no frills, and I'm sure she will look beautiful in it."

Wallis caught himself nodding. She would indeed. He cleared his throat and tried to look stern. He had a feeling a silly grin was on his face.

"Shall I take these two to the counter?" Alma asked. She grabbed the pink one back off the rack and held it up with the purple one. "Or do you want to look around a bit more?"

What he wanted was to beat his head against a wall. Instead, he nodded again, and tried to look stern by rubbing his chin. "Yes, she'd look good in these two, especially the pink …" Though his heart was telling him to buy all of them. Dash it all. "But I didn't come in here to buy Jean dresses. I came in to look at fabric for curtains for the library and Jean's place. Can you hold everything we picked out until tomorrow?"

Alma sighed with disappointment and put the dresses back on the rack. "Yes, of course."

"Thank you. Jean and I will be by tomorrow and she can decide which items she likes best." He headed for the double doors.

"Mr. Darling ..."

He stopped and turned. "Yes, Alma?"

She looked at the floor. "I know it's none of my business. But Jean ... she hides her pain."

He stepped toward her. "What do you mean?"

"Understand. Jean didn't have to deal with only her father's death, but with everyone's. I think that maybe ..." She looked at him. "... Jean hasn't grieved yet."

Wallis stared at her in shock. "How do you know this?"

She shrugged. "Because ..." She let go a nervous laugh. "I'm good at pretending everything's all right when it's not. That makes it easy to recognize when someone else is doing it too."

Wallis was quiet for a moment. He hadn't thought of Jean that way – or Alma, come to that. He cleared his throat. "Any help I can give her ..."

Alma nodded. "Just be there for her if she, you know, has a moment of grief. I only say this because when we had to bury everyone, I never saw her cry. She was too busy. Since then, we've all been going about our daily lives. But of all of us, she has the least to do. Fixing up the library and her place together might help her."

Wallis nodded in understanding, then smiled gratefully. "Thank you, Alma. I'll remember that."

He stepped out the door and realized he never once

asked Jean about losing her father. Had she grieved in private, and no one knew the depths of her despair? Or was Alma right, and she had yet to mourn?

He pondered this as he crossed the street to the hotel. He planned on helping her with the library and fixing up her little home. But maybe he could also help her broken heart. He just had to find the courage to do it. To let her cry, rant, and rave, even scream. And if she got angry, he'd need the patience to let it pass and not try to fix it. Just be a listening ear and be there for her.

But for him, that was a tall order. He couldn't stand the sight of a crying woman. He didn't know what to do with himself. What man did?

He shook the thought off as he entered the hotel. Should he ask Dora about this? Then again, it was Jean's private business. Alma should never have told him. But if she knew, did Dora? And what about Letty?

Out of curiosity, he went into the kitchen. Dora was at the stove taking something out of the oven. "You're just in time," she said. She put a pan of roast chicken on the worktable, then bent to the oven again and pulled out another.

He ignored the delicious smell and sight of the food. "Dora, may I ask you something?"

"Sure, Wallis." She set the hot pad down next to the pans and wiped her hands on her apron. "What is it?"

He took a deep breath. "It's probably none of my ... that is, it *isn't* any of my business. But ... when the incident happened, did ... Jean cry a lot?"

She exhaled and shook her head.

His breath hitched. "Not at all?"

"Not in public." She picked up a hot pad and shoved one pan toward a large platter. "At the funerals we cried. All of us. But Jean was busy trying to take care of everyone. Though we didn't bury all at the same time. Cassie's father, for instance"

"Yes, I heard that."

"But there was the day we buried six, including Jean's father."

He stared at her. "How dreadful."

Dora nodded. "Indeed, it was. That day was unbearable for everyone including Jean, but she put on a brave face. She didn't cry once that I saw. Just bowed her head and tried not to look."

He sighed. "Alma said Jean hasn't fully grieved. What do you think?"

Dora looked away and wrung her hands in her apron. "I think Jean buried her grief deep down and locked it away. Until she's ready to confront it, I'm afraid she'll continue to pretend it's not there." She met his eyes. "We all wish she would open up. But I think it's too painful for her to do that. She's too strong to break down completely."

He smiled sadly, knowing what Dora said was true. With a nod of appreciation, he headed for the door. "Thank you."

He left the kitchen with a heavy heart and swore he could feel the sorrow radiating from Dora. He wanted to help Jean grieve, but he didn't know how. Maybe the best thing he could do was be there for her if something caused her to break down. Though he had no idea what that might be.

Wallis straightened his shoulders. He had a new mission now, one he was determined to fulfill. There was a strong chance he'd not have to deal with any of it. But if he did, he was determined to be ready.

Jean waited in front of the library. It was almost ten o'clock. Mr. Atkins would bring the lumber any moment now.

"Good morning," Wallis greeted her as he joined her.

Her belly flipped. "Morning." Oh, no – she wasn't that attracted to him, was she?

"After Mr. Atkins and I unload the wagon and get everything inside, I want you to take a pencil and mark where you think the shelves should go. As soon as I'm done working at Sarah's place, I'll return here and start putting them up. I also picked out a few things for your place and the library at Alma's before dinner last night."

She smiled. "You didn't."

He bowed. "I admit I lack Phileas' flair for decorating. But I have decent taste."

She smiled and looked him over. Today he wore a simple blue bandanna around his neck and a light brown jacket over dark trousers. He'd combed his dark hair well off his face, which had a pleasant openness that gave her a sense of comfort. "I'm sure whatever you picked out will be perfect." She sat on the bench by the door, and he joined her.

While they waited, he shared stories about his travels, the books he'd read, and the library. As they talked, Jean realized just how much Wallis wanted to help the library succeed. His passion for books and knowledge was as compelling as his charming personality. He was the perfect person to help her bring the library to life.

As soon as Mr. Atkins showed up, they got to work. She helped the men unload the shelves and discussed the best places to hang them. Before Wallis left, she marked the walls as he instructed, and the two of them moved some shelves closer to the wall they'd start with.

She tried to imagine the finished shelves and pictured the two of them stepping back to admire their work. But when her imagination had Wallis take her by the hand, she squeezed her eyes shut. No, no, no!

"Something wrong?" he asked.

Jean smiled. "Something in my eye." She opened them and looked around with satisfaction. "I'm sure this will be an enormous success."

"Thanks to us," Wallis said, looking proud.

"Thanks to you," she corrected. "You and Mr. Atkins did most of the work. I couldn't have done this by myself."

He blushed and looked away. "It was nothing."

Jean smiled and had a strong feeling she could get

used to having him around. She couldn't afford to get attached, though. He was probably leaving in a week or two.

"I must be going," he said cheerfully. "Go to Alma's, look at what I picked out. And once you have, do me a favor?"

She smiled. "What's that?"

"If you hate my choices, don't tell me. Just have Alma put everything back, then pick out what you want." He put on his hat, tipped it, then headed for the door.

She giggled and tried to ignore the giddiness in her belly. She felt good when she was with him and wasn't sure what to do about it. Her heart had been empty for too long; did she dare let him get a foothold? He wasn't what she'd expected, for one. The Darling brothers were British, and she, like so many others, thought they'd be stuffy, boring, stoic. But that wasn't the case. Instead, they were more than helpful, funny, and attentive. Wallis, in particular, was bold and surprisingly charming.

Jean made sure the marks for the shelves were in the right places, then took what books she had and organized them. As she worked, she thought of Wallis and the way her heart raced when she was with him this morning. As much as she wanted to deny it, she was drawn to the Englishman. Should she use this time to get to know him better and see what else they had in common? After all, he was leaving soon, and she'd probably never see him again. Maybe they could write?

Besides, like his idea of a fake courtship, what could it hurt for just a few days?

She pushed the thought aside and went to the general store. Alma was quick to show her Wallis' pile of goods. "He leans towards solid patterns," Alma said. "But I know you like things more colorful."

Jean looked over the folded fabric, rugs, and lace. She fingered the latter and held it up. "Did he pick this thinking I could trim the curtains with it?"

"I would think so. I doubt he thought you could trim the rugs."

Jean laughed. "Let's hope not." She studied the pile again. "You're right, some of this is too plain. Let's pick out something with flowers." She shoved the small pile of fabric to one side, spied a pretty vase on a top shelf and pointed at it. "Add that, would you?"

"I will." Alma sauntered to the clothes rack. "He did have good taste when it came to dresses."

She followed her. "What?"

Alma pulled a few frocks off the rack. "I showed him these yesterday, and he thought you would look lovely in them."

She gasped. "Alma, you didn't."

"Why not? He's sweet on you, isn't he?" She put the dresses back and grinned.

Jean fought the urge to bury her face in her hands. Okay, so Alma thought they were courting. Or ... "He really said that?"

She smiled and nodded. "He even liked the hat that goes with the brown dress."

Jean eyed the dress she'd picked out yesterday and sighed. "Well, he didn't buy any of them, now did he?"

"No, which puzzles me." Alma went to a shelf and started pulling off bolts of fabric. "I mean, if a man is sweet on a girl, shouldn't he buy her a few nice things?" She brought the fabric to the counter and set it down. "What about these?"

Jean looked at the flowered fabric. "Much better."

"Have you measured the windows of the library yet?"

"No, but I can do that now." She stroked one corner of a pretty yellow fabric with tiny flowers. "So ... did he say anything else?"

Alma stared at her a moment before looking down. "No. Nothing. He just remarked about the dresses. You should go measure."

Jean's eyebrows shot up. Was she trying to get rid of her? That was so unlike the young woman. Normally you couldn't get away – Alma talked nonstop.

She shrugged and made her way back to the library. Thoughts of Wallis flooded her mind, and she sighed. Maybe he was sweet on her, and maybe he wasn't. All she knew was that she looked forward to seeing him again.

As she entered the library, she vowed not to let her heart get carried away. This was a courtship of convenience (if even that) and if he left in a week, she'd be none the worse for wear. But she couldn't stop wondering what it would be like if this were more than playacting.

What if it were real? What if they allowed themselves to admit the feelings (if any) they had for each other?

Jean squared her shoulders, determined not to get lost in such foolish thoughts. She didn't need a stroll down Stupid Street.

But as she concentrated on measuring the windows for the library, a small smile tugged at the corner of her lips. No matter what she told herself, she realized she'd been hoping for something more than a courtship of convenience. She also couldn't help but wonder what Wallis was really thinking. Was he being serious when he looked at those dresses with Alma, or just trying to pull her into his little scheme?

It was fun to think of him as being sweet on her. But why would he be? He was leaving soon, after all. Besides, Alma was prone to exaggeration.

Her heart sank as she wrote down the measurements and headed back to the store. She had to stop thinking about him that way. If her heart got away from her, it was setting her up for more pain, and she'd had enough the day she buried a half-dozen men.

Jean made a new pile of goods, left them with Alma (who reminded her Wallis was paying) and returned to the library. She needed to make a list of everyone in town that might have books to donate. She'd like a variety for the library and jotted some titles down as well.

There was Emily Bronte's *Wuthering Heights* and Jane Austen's *Pride and Prejudice* (nothing like a classic) and the collection of poetry from Lord Byron would be nice. But she also wanted something more like Mark Twain's *The Adventures of Huckleberry Finn*. There was also *Twilight of Pioneers* by Betsy Ross, *In the Heart of the Wild* by Henry David Thoreau, *The Lady of the Lake* by Sir Walter Scott, and *Gulliver's Travels* by Jonathan Swift.

As she wrote the titles, she couldn't help but daydream about Wallis. His smile and his wit would make her library a better place. Sure, everyone in town might have books to donate, but nothing as nice as what Wallis was bringing in. It was just a shame that he would be gone so soon.

Once she was done, she took a moment to look around the library. This wasn't the life she'd expected, but it was the one she had, and it was a decent life. She could do a lot of good for the townsfolk and the library was a place for joy and learning.

She should be thankful for her blessings. For instance, she was lucky to have Wallis in her life, even if it was only for a few more days. It was nice having someone so considerate and she knew she'd always remember him.

No matter what happened, Jean was grateful for their time together, because he had been a bright spot during a difficult time. She had little money, and he'd helped her follow an idea and see it through. She didn't have his confidence, and he'd given it to her in spades. Though what would happen to that confidence when he was gone?

Chapter Eight

Wallis headed back to town with his brothers. They finished tearing out the floor, got the ground turned underneath to help get rid of any remaining odor, and started on the new floor. They'd have it done tomorrow with all of them working, and then it was Jean's turn.

Speaking of Jean ... "I say, but is that Billy Watson with a wheelbarrow of books?" Phileas asked.

"It is," Irving observed. "And Jean's with him." He glanced at Wallis. "Looks like they've been collecting for the library."

Wallis smiled. "Indeed, it does. If you'll excuse me, I'd like to see what they've rounded up." He increased his stride and waved at them.

"Hi, Mr. Darling!" Billy called.

"Good afternoon, young man," Wallis said as he

approached. "My, what do we have here?" He nodded at the wheelbarrow.

"I've been helping Miss Campbell get books for the library," Billy said. "It's the least I can do considering I'll never go in there."

Jean smiled. "He's made that quite clear, trust me."

Wallis arched an eyebrow at the boy. "What do you mean, you won't go into the library?"

Billy pressed his lips together and shook his head. "I don't read."

"But you're in school," Wallis argued.

"I'll read in school." Billy crossed his arms and made another face. "I hate reading. Unless it's an adventure book. Then I like it."

He picked up a book on gardening. "Well, not all books have adventure in them." He put it back and picked up another. This one was some sort of philosophy book. "But that doesn't mean Jean can't get her hands on the sort of books you like."

Billy's eyes rounded to saucers as he looked at her. "Is that true?"

"Sure is," she said. "I can order a lot of things for the library. I just need the funds."

Billy's face fell. "Oh, money." He made another face as he eyed them both. "How come money gets in the way of things?"

Wallis shrugged. "You mean the lack of it."

"Yeah, I guess I do. My Pa says money is the root of all evil."

"If used unwisely, it can be," Wallis said. "But I see it as a tool."

Billy sighed. "For what?"

"Well, getting books for the library, for instance. Jean can look at books in a catalogue, pick some out, add up the total cost, and know how much money she'll need to purchase them. Then she can set a goal when she'd like to have the money."

Billy shook his head as if he was about to correct a naughty child. "Everyone knows that."

"Yes, which is why it's what Jean will do. Then she can figure out how to raise the money to get the books."

"I know that too," Billy said as if bored.

Wallis winked at Jean. "And if you help her, the sooner she can order those adventure books for the library."

Billy's eyes darted between them. "Ohh."

"Mm-hmm," Jean said. "So, are you going to help me again?"

Billy made another face. "Well, today was lucky. You had a lot of books you were carrying, and I have my ma's wheelbarrow."

Jean tried not to smile. "Yes, wasn't I lucky to have run into you?"

"Then I tagged along," Billy said. "Before we knew it, we had all these books." He stared at the pile. "Do you think there's an adventure tale in there?"

"Could be," she drawled. "Why don't we take these to the library and find out?"

Billy perused the pile of books like it was a platter of fried chicken. "If there is, can I take it home and read it?" He straightened. "That would make me your first customer."

She put a hand over her mouth and snorted. "Yes, it would."

"But you said you wouldn't set foot in the library," Wallis pointed out.

"For a good adventure I will. Does the captain know yet?"

"Yes," Jean said. "He gave me a few books. They're at the bottom. If you help me unload these, you can have your pick."

He smiled and took off.

"Where is he going?" Wallis asked.

"The library," she laughed. "Where else?"

"He's a precocious child, isn't he?"

"Billy's curious, about everything. And not afraid to speak his mind."

"That, I've heard." He gently pushed her away from the wheelbarrow and got it moving. "My, this is heavy. You should have waited for me."

"Nonsense, I had help."

He laughed. "Billy was letting you do all the work."

She bit her lip as her eyebrows shot up. Finally she shook her head. "He's the reason I got all these books."

His own eyebrows rose. "Do tell?"

"He's a born salesman. I doubt I'd have collected half as many books without him. His own father donated a brand-new book and said he wanted to be the first one to check it out."

Wallis laughed. "Goodness gracious."

"I think it was the only way to get Billy to leave."

Wallis laughed some more. "He knocked on his own door to collect books?"

"It was our first stop. He insisted."

Wallis walked slowly, wishing they weren't so close to the library. It was a pleasant evening, and he enjoyed talking with her. "Jean ..."

She smiled at him.

"After we unload the books, why not join us for dinner?"

To his surprise she stopped. "Oh, I ... don't know."

"Why not? Do you have other plans?"

She glanced at the hotel, then the general store across the street. "I picked some things out. Alma is holding them."

"Jolly good. Now about dinner ..."

She sighed. Did she not want to eat with him? "I ... all right."

He cocked his head. "Are you not feeling well? Would you rather be alone?"

She looked at the ground. "I'm fine. It's ... this has been exciting and wonderful and scary ..."

"Indeed."

She looked at him. "And you're here. Doing it all with me."

"I am." What could be wrong? Did she not want his help?

"Wallis ... it's been nice having your help." She blushed.

He smiled as his chest swelled. "I'm glad to do it. Now let's take care of these books, shall we?"

They met Billy at the library and went inside. Between the three of them, they could sort the books into stacks, and luckily for Billy there were six adventure books. *The Tiger Hunter* by Mayne Reid intrigued the boy the most, so Jean let him "check it out." "Oh boy!" Billy held the book and stared at the cover.

"Are you sure you can read that?" Wallis asked.

Billy grinned. "Oh, I'm not going to read it. I'm going to have the captain read it to me."

Wallis smiled. "I see. And when will this happen?"

"The next time we meet in the crow's nest. That's where we have our lessons."

Jean smiled at him. "Billy, why don't you pick out a book that you can read."

"But then it will be for ..." He looked sheepish. "Babies."

"Babies can't read," Wallis pointed out. "They're, well, babies."

"I mean a child," Billy said with an eye roll.

It was all Wallis could do not to laugh. "But you are a child."

"I'm seven. Practically a man, according to some."

He exchanged a look of amusement with Jean. "And who is that?"

"Flint. His pa died, so he's the man of his house and he's younger than I am."

Wallis nodded. "But he won't be the man of the house for much longer."

"Yeah, I heard about that." Billy held his book close to his chest. "Can I help with the library?"

Jean smiled. "That's kind of you to offer, Billy. But I'm not sure what you can do."

"I can think of a few things," Wallis said. "I hear you're a good worker."

"Conrad told you, didn't he?"

"He certainly did, and a few other things too." He smiled at Jean who smiled back. "I also heard you like to go fishing."

Billy's eyes lit up. "I do! Would you like to go?"

"Well, maybe." He smiled again and glanced at Jean. "Would you like to come along?"

Billy gasped. "You want her to come?"

"Why not?" he asked. "Maybe she'd like to fish too."

Billy frowned and shook his head. "Well, just so long as you remember what happened to your brother when he went fishing with Sheriff Cassie."

"And what was that?" Jean asked.

"They fell in love and *kissed*," Billy said, aghast.

That did it. Wallis burst into laughter.

"It's true!" Billy said over his guffaws. "Ask anyone!"

"We believe you," Jean said. "I'll be extra careful if I ever go fishing with Mr. Darling."

"You'd better," Billy said with relief. "Or you'll get hitched before you know it." He clutched the book tighter and headed for the door. "My ma will be looking for me, so I'd better go." He turned to face them. "But I'll be back tomorrow. What time do you want me?"

Wallis exchanged another look with Jean. "It's up to Miss Campbell."

"How about ten?" she said. "If you don't have any other pressing engagements."

"No, I'm free." Billy opened the door. "I'll see you then."

He left, and as soon as he was well away, they both laughed. "That boy!" Jean said through her giggles. "He expects to be paid, just so you know."

"I know." He looked at her, a smile on his face, then offered his arm. "To dinner?"

She looked at the arm, gulped, then took it.

Wallis swallowed hard, his heart pounding, and it wasn't from their recent bout of laughter. This was because of Jean.

🫖

At the hotel, not all the brothers were in attendance. Sterling was at Letty's along with Sarah and her children. It made for a quiet meal and Jean stole tiny glances at Wallis throughout dinner. Every time he caught her, her heart skipped and her belly flipped. If this kept up, she didn't know what she'd do.

Should she be spending time with him at all? Worse, when it came time for him and his brothers to leave, would the hole left behind by her father's death widen? Right now, Wallis was filling it with shovelfuls of attention, charm, and no small amount of kindness. How much more could she take before she didn't want him to leave?

A chill went up her spine. Her heart had disappeared for the longest time. She felt nothing after she buried her father along with the rest. It was as if her heart no longer existed. She hadn't been able to feel much since. No sensations of pain other than a tiny twinge now and then. She knew it wasn't normal but wouldn't argue with it either. She liked not having to feel.

But this ... she wasn't sure what Wallis was doing to her. Despite the state of her heart, when he looked at her, she sensed something beyond her control, like the way his eyes held her and made her feel uncomfortable yet strangely alive. He'd awoken something within her she'd been too numb to feel before. The mixture of emotions slowly rising were strange and powerful. And they terrified her.

"I forgot to ask," Wallis said softly.

He sat next to her, and it was hard not to lean closer to him. She could feel the heat radiating off his body and liked it. "What?"

"Did you get by Alma's?"

Another delicious chill went up her spine, and she did her best not to move. "Yes."

"And?"

Jean looked at him, saw the curiosity in his eyes and smiled. "She put some things back." She grinned.

"Oh, I see." He not only smiled but blushed as well. "I told you I was no Phileas."

"What's that?" Phileas said from across the table.

"Nothing." Wallis winked at her. "What did you pick out?"

"Well, for the curtains for my bedroom, I chose a nice yellow fabric with little flowers. Alma recommended a few shelves for my wall – that is, if we have any left over. She thought I could stain some a medium-dark color that would match the dresser I already have."

Wallis nodded and smiled. "That sounds perfect."

"Yes, I think so too." Jean smiled, feeling a little bashful. It was nice to know Wallis wasn't upset by her changing his selections. "I was also lucky enough to find a pretty vase. I thought it might look good in my front room."

"Indeed." His eyes twinkled with admiration. "I can't wait to see it."

This time she couldn't help but shiver as little tingles assailed her. What was happening? They were talking about curtains and vases, for crying out loud.

He smiled, his gaze saturating her with warmth. "Now, what other ideas do you have? Did you pick out anything else?"

She forced her gaze away and tried to concentrate on her food. But there was something between them, and she knew it. "I think..." she swallowed hard, her words emerging as a whisper, "I think we should paint the baseboards a warm color."

He leaned closer and to her surprise, brushed a stray lock of hair behind her ear. She looked at him and held her breath, unable to move as his eyes bored into hers. She felt suspended in time and space, her heart pounding in her chest, waiting for something to happen. For what seemed like forever, they sat, eyes locked together, as Dora went to fetch dessert. What was happening?!

"Dora made a cherry pie," he whispered.

She nodded, not trusting her voice. As he moved away, she touched her hair, still feeling the brush of his finger against her cheek. Whatever just happened had been far more powerful than anything she'd ever experienced before. And all he did was get some hair out of her face!

She should have stayed home and had a can of beans for dinner.

Dora returned with two pies, Phileas right behind her. She didn't even notice he'd left the room. Jean put her hand to her chest, hoping to still her heart, but it was no good. She was feeling things she'd never experienced before.

Drat Wallis Darling! What was she going to do? She couldn't act on her emotions. She'd wind up with a broken heart and then what?

Jean stared at the few bites of roast chicken left on her plate and took a few moments to compose herself. She'd have to keep her emotions in check for the rest of the evening and try to put some distance between them. She could strike up a conversation with Dora or Phileas about the hotel or ask if she could take a tray up to poor Oliver. Last she heard, he was upstairs reading, and that Dora had set something aside for him.

She also had to concede that Wallis was a kind, intelligent gentleman and she was lucky to have him in her life, however briefly. She clung to that thought, resolved to enjoy their time together as they worked on the library. Surely she could put up with a few days of "feeling" things. Then again ...

Taking a bite of the chicken, she decided that after dinner, she'd thank Dora for the meal, then run home and get as far away from Wallis's intoxicating presence as she could. Because right now, she wasn't sure she could stand another minute of it. He was so, so ... oh, for Pete's sake. Why did this have to happen?

"Are you all right?" he asked. "You look flushed."

She fought an eye roll. Was it any wonder? For the first time in her life, a man had her attention. Unfortunately, this one wasn't sticking around. She had a dream, a life that included a husband and family. None of which she could have with Wallis Darling. Besides, even if she was getting sweet on him, he'd shown no signs of being sweet on her. So what if he stuck some hair behind her ear? She was lucky she didn't shove it into her mouth while she was eating. How embarrassing would that be?

"Jean?"

She jumped. "What?"

"You're ... staring at nothing," he breathed. "I dare say, you look a million miles away."

She forced a smile. She might as well be. "It's nothing. I was thinking about the vase I picked out."

"I'd like to see it. Flowers always brighten up a room. My mother loves them and there's no shortage of blooms in our house."

"I can only imagine. Your mother must miss you." She looked around the table. "All of you."

"I'm sure she does," Conrad said. "But she knows ..." His eyes skipped from one brother to the next. "... our expected return date."

"And when is that?" she asked.

Wallis leaned toward her again and, her heart skipped. "Not for a while. And we need to finish what we started here."

"I can handle the library."

"Nonsense," he said. "I said I'd help you with it and I shall."

"I can help," Conrad volunteered.

"I would offer," Phileas said. "But somebody already drafted me for it."

She giggled. "Thank you, all of you."

"I'm pleased to speak for Sterling and Irving," Conrad said. "They'll be happy to help too."

She laughed. "Thank you. Between all of you, the library will be done in no time."

"And your place?" Dora prompted.

"Is not as important as the library," she said.

Wallis poked at his pie. "You have a few bad floorboards, remember?"

"Oh, those." She reached for her coffee cup. "But let's take care of the library first." Working on the library wasn't as personal as her living quarters. For one, the library was for everyone to enjoy. "Billy's going to help us," she announced.

"Billy?" Conrad said with a grin. "You realize he expects to get paid?"

"We know," Wallis said. "I'll take care of it." He smiled at Jean, took another bite of his pie, and gazed into her eyes a moment.

Jean swallowed hard, reached for another piece, and hoped it was enough to distract her.

Chapter Nine

What was he doing? Wallis could kick himself for being so forward with Jean. True, all he did was brush a lock of hair off her face. Heaven forbid she got it tangled in her mashed potatoes. But when he locked eyes with her, it was almost more than he could bear.

It was bad enough seeing how kind she was, but when he heard about how she put others' needs before her own ... well, if he stayed long enough, they would eventually find their way to each other. But he wasn't staying, and that was that.

And yet, as Wallis stared into her eyes over dessert, his heart raced faster than ever, and he fought the urge to lean her way. Like a moth to a flame, she drew him. He tried to shake it off and focus on the conversation about the library but couldn't look away. Thank goodness he had some pie left and could take bites to distract himself.

"Wallis," Dora said. "Would you mind taking a plate up to Oliver?"

"Not at all." He followed her into the kitchen.

She gave him a coy look. "So, I noticed you were rather attentive to Jean this evening."

"Really?" He caught the smug look on her face and stared at the worktable, as if deep in thought.

"If I didn't know any better," Dora said with a smile "I'd say you were getting sweet on her."

Wallis tried to ignore the heat crawling up his neck. "I'm just helping Jean out with the library."

"Mm-hmm," Dora said knowingly. "Sure you are." She handed him a plate of food. "Take this to Oliver."

Wallis took the plate, his entire face on fire. He knew if he stayed in Apple Blossom any longer, he would end up falling for Jean. But as he had to return to England, what could he do?

He tried not to think about it as he left the kitchen and trudged up the stairs to Oliver. Once there, he knocked and waited. When Oliver answered the door, he took one look at him and laughed. "What did you do? Run here?" He peered at the plate. "Roast chicken, how lovely." He took it and stepped back. "Your eyes aren't watering. I must not smell as bad this evening."

Wallis shrugged. "Perhaps not." He clasped his hands behind his back and began to pace.

"Whatever is the matter?" Oliver sniffed at the chicken.

He stopped pacing. "It's nothing." He tried to keep

his face from reddening again, but it was no use. His cheeks felt like firecrackers.

Oliver chuckled and waved him into the room. "Come sit down. I won't bite."

Wallis stepped inside. The stench wasn't as bad as the day before. He was glad he wasn't the one to have a run-in with a skunk. Then again, if he had been, he might not be getting sweet on Jean. He took a seat on the edge of Oliver's bed and looked at the sparse furnishings, the small dresser in one corner and a lone chair across from it. The walls were bare but for a few books scattered about, the titles of which Wallis couldn't make out.

"So," Oliver said. "How goes the work on the library and Jean's place?"

Wallis sighed. "It's coming along, but it's not finished yet." He ran his hand through his hair. "Jean is a hard worker and seems to have found her calling as the new town librarian. She's excited about opening it." He paused and looked at his brother. "But the library needs more books, and Jean could use all the help she can get if we're to get it finished by the time we leave." He paused again and his eyes softened. For a moment, he was inclined to stay. But that couldn't happen. "I hope she has help with it after we're gone."

Oliver gave him a knowing smile and patted him on the shoulder. "You're doing a great service for the town, as well as helping Jean. She's been through a lot, just like so many others."

Wallis nodded thoughtfully and stood. He didn't

want to burden his brother with his current challenge. It would send poor Ollie into a panic. "I'll leave you to your dinner." He forced a smile. "Good night." Without another word he stepped out and headed for the stairs, his mind on his "challenge". If he stayed in Apple Blossom any longer, he would inevitably have to choose between his heart and England. And how could he do that?

He was returning to England in a little over a week if all went well, and he had to remain focused on the tasks at hand. There was just one problem — how could he work on the library and everything else and stay away from Jean? It was impossible. He'd just have to keep his heart in check. Maybe he should look up the skunk that sprayed Oliver.

Tonight it felt like a jolt of lightning had surged through him. He'd grown attached to Jean in such a short period and kept telling himself there wasn't any point in getting attached at all. Their lives were taking them in different directions and soon enough they'd have to go their own ways. His fear was, that every day spent with Jean would bring new feelings toward her, ones that would become too strong for him ignore.

But despite his undeniable attraction to her, Wallis couldn't help but think about his looming departure. He'd already made plans of what he'd do his first few weeks back in England and knew he wouldn't stay here.

Worse, if he acted on his attraction, he would still have to return home without her ... or worse, take her away from everyone she loved in Apple Blossom. The thought of being so selfish would keep him awake at night and paralyze him during his remaining days with Jean – moments that were too precious to waste, yet doomed from the start because of an uncertain future. Dash it all!

Why did there have to be something special between them? Whether they were discussing books in the library or walking around town sharing stories of their pasts, he was experiencing a deep connection unlike anything he'd experienced before. But to what end? He didn't think he was falling in love the way his brothers had. He had growing feelings, yes, but would he propose to Jean tomorrow? No. For all he knew, it was her love of books that drew him.

He'd focus on going home. Until then, he'd savor what little time they had left in this magical town before returning to England ... possibly with one brother – an outcome that seemed more likely than ever before. Thank goodness Oliver got sprayed by that skunk or he might wind up losing his heart to someone too.

He went back into the hotel and caught Dora and Phileas at a table in the dining room. They were sipping coffee, talking, and smiling at each other. Should he break it up? He watched them, transfixed. Was a romantic spark forming between the two?

Phileas saw him and waved. "Wallis, are you heading up?"

He stepped into the dining room. "I see you've

found an extra cherry pie." He eyed the pair. "Is that what the two of you are smiling about?"

Dora had the decency to look guilty. "Um, well ..."

Phileas just looked sheepish. "She hid it."

Wallis laughed. He knew Dora was always up for a sneak snack. "Well, I'm glad you found it before I did," he said with a wink. "Who knows what kind of trouble we'd be in if I'd gotten my hands on it?"

"We? You mean you," Dora said. "You're the one that would get a bellyache. But I'm sorry. If I don't hide the goodies, they might be gone before morning. I don't know who's raiding the kitchen in the middle of the night, but so far this week the cookie jar's become empty, half a loaf of bread is missing, and the last two pieces of apple pie from last night disappeared."

"Don't look at me," he said. "But I can guess who it is." He glanced between them, his eyes settling on Phileas. "Oliver," they said at once.

"Oh, poor man," Dora said. "He ought to bathe again tomorrow. I think it's helping."

Wallis chuckled and nodded in agreement. "All right, I'll talk to him when I go upstairs. I think it's time for me to get some rest."

"I should go up too," Phileas said. He smiled at Dora, drained his cup and stood. "Until tomorrow."

Dora waved at him. "Good night."

Wallis looked for any sign of attraction between them. Maybe he was wrong, and he was imagining things. Thank goodness for that. He was having a hard enough time fighting his attraction to Jean. The last thing he needed was for Phileas to look at Dora as something more than a pretty fixture in the hotel.

Jean awoke the next day with books on her mind. She got up, washed, dressed, ate a quick breakfast and headed for the library. She wanted to organize the books she collected with Billy. Once the shelves were up, she could start adding books to them. She'd have to get the categories sorted, and the books organized alphabetically in each one. This could be an all-day project seeing as how she'd have to write the name of each book on an index card, then assign it a category and number.

When she arrived at the library, Wallis was waiting. "Good morning," he greeted her. "Are you ready to get to work?"

She took a deep breath and smiled. "As ready as I'll ever be." Her eyes roamed over him, and she cleared her throat, embarrassed by her bold perusal. But he was so darn handsome, and she remembered the brush of his finger against her cheek as he swept her hair away. "We'd better get to work." She unlocked the door, and they went inside.

"My brothers will join us shortly. We'll get the shelves up, then I'll help you with the books."

She smiled as her cheeks heated. Again. She hoped

someone would be along soon. They could act as chaperone.

When his brothers arrived, the work went quickly. Wallis was the most skilled with the tools, and he gave directions to the others. Jean watched him in awe, feeling a strange warmth in her chest. "You're very precise with a hammer," she commented when he started on another shelf.

"I helped my father a lot with repairs. More than the rest, I suppose."

"Billy will be jealous." The boy arrived recently, disappointed no one had waited to start work until he got there. "He's good with a hammer too. For a seven-year-old."

"He got a lot of practice working on Cassie's house." He held a bracket against the wall. "Hold this, will you?"

She did as he hammered a nail into it. When he was done, he smiled at her. "Thank you."

She blushed and smiled back. "You're welcome." She turned away, fanned herself with her hand and hoped none of his brothers noticed her heated cheeks. In the short time since Wallis arrived, his hands had become rough and calloused from all the hard work he'd done. She watched with awe as he hammered, his arms flexing. He wore well-worn jeans, the sleeves of his white shirt rolled up, and his shoes had tracked dirt on the floor.

Her eyes traveled from his hand holding the next nail, up his arm to his shoulder, then to his chest. His breathing was soft and even as he worked, his grunts and sighs as he exerted himself like a song Jean had never heard before. Worse, her nostrils filled with the strong, spicy smell of him mixed with sweat. It should have been offensive, but it wasn't.

Jean fanned herself harder. Okay, so she was more than a little attracted to him. Not that it was going to do her a lick of good when he left. She sighed and pushed her feelings aside. There was no use getting attached to him. She had no choice but to put the attraction out of her mind and focus on the work before her. She grabbed some books from a pile she'd organized earlier and stacked them neatly onto the shelf that Wallis had finished hammering together.

His brothers moved around, taking turns with the tools, helping each other out, laughing, teasing; she felt as if she was invading an exclusive club. They glanced in her direction now and then but never said a word or came close enough for conversation. She knew each had things on their minds and were preoccupied. Sterling, Conrad, and Irving were getting married. Phileas was probably thinking about the hotel. Oliver, well, he wasn't there.

Jean worked silently and tried to steer her mind away from distracting thoughts. It was easier to focus on the books, assigning them categories and numbers. She wrote them all down on the index cards and began placing them onto the shelves.

She'd almost finished her third shelf when Wallis appeared. He glanced around, admiration in his eyes. "You've done a great job."

"Thanks," she said, warmth blooming in her chest.

"My brothers and I couldn't have done it without your help."

She looked up and smiled. His gaze held hers for a few seconds and for the first time that day she was hit with something more than simple attraction.

He smiled back and picked up a few nails from the floor. Jean watched him, a chill running up her spine. She hadn't realized she'd come to care for Wallis. She was going to have to handle this or risk a broken heart.

She got back to work and smiled without looking at him, her cheeks burning even more at the knowledge that he watched her. She grabbed another book and concentrated on cataloguing it. But her thoughts scattered, and her skin tingled with awareness each time his gaze lingered on her. Doggone it! What was she going to do?

Jean pushed aside the longing that threatened and returned her attention to the books, her fingers tracing them like gentle caresses. She knew Wallis watched her, intrigued by her fingers moving along the spines of the books like a skilled musician along the keys of the piano. She liked the feel of the spines and bindings and tried to focus on that. Maybe if she ignored him, he'd go away. Or ... Jean smiled. "Billy, come here."

The boy came running. "Yes, Miss Campbell, you need something?"

Jean glanced at Wallis, who was but feet away. "Do the shelves look straight to you?"

He crossed his skinny arms over his chest and narrowed his eyes at them. "Look okay to me."

"Of course, they're straight," Wallis said. "We measured everything perfectly."

She smiled weakly. "So we did." Okay, this wasn't working. "We should break for lunch."

"Jolly good idea," Conrad said. "I'm starved." He set his hammer aside and headed for the door. "I'm sure Dora has made something."

"Jean, Billy," Wallis said. "Would you like to join us?"

"I would," Billy chimed, eyes bright. "Let's go!" He ran after Conrad.

She sighed and looked at Wallis. Would he follow them now too?

He smiled at her before walking off with his brothers – a sad smile, as if disappointed they were finished.

Jean shook her head as she realized how much she would miss him even if she didn't allow herself to do something stupid like fall in love.

When they reached the hotel, everyone gathered in the kitchen, where Dora was setting out sandwiches and lemonade. Jean's mouth watered when she saw the spread; she'd been too busy thinking about Wallis to notice she was hungry.

The men headed out back to wash up while Billy lingered at the back door. "What kind of sandwiches did you make?"

Dora smiled at him. "Roast beef. Hungry?"

Billy nodded enthusiastically, then ran out back to

join the men. Dora made him a plate before turning to Jean with a questioning look.

Jean was about to tell her she was more than ready to eat when Wallis re-entered the kitchen. "I hope you're hungry," he said, his eyes steadied on hers.

She swallowed hard and took a seat at the table. Here it was again, a warm sensation in her heart that also flooded her face. How was she supposed to make it through lunch?

His brothers joined them, the blessing said, and everyone began to eat.

Jean took a bite of her sandwich, more than aware that everyone glanced her way now and then in silence. Her face must be beet red. She concentrated on eating instead of meeting their curious gazes, taking extra effort to avoid Wallis'. He sat across the table from her with Billy, and she swore she could feel his eyes on her.

When they finished eating, Wallis stood and cleared his throat before addressing everyone. "We still have work to do," he said authoritatively. "Let's get back to it." He gave Jean one last lingering glance before leaving the kitchen with the others in tow.

She watched him go, relieved he was leaving, but disappointed that nothing happened beyond an intimate exchange of glances and a few brief words.

What Jean should be feeling was grateful. If a few words and glances could turn her into a mindless puddle, what would happen if by some miracle he kissed her?

Chapter Ten

Wallis tried not to watch Jean during lunch, but it was hard. Thank Heaven, it was attraction and nothing more. At least that's what he kept telling himself.

They returned to the library and cleaned up their work areas. They still had to build another middle shelf unit and secure it. If they worked the rest of the afternoon, they might get it done.

"Mr. Darling?" Billy asked.

Wallis grabbed his hammer. "Hmm?"

"Why does the town have to have a dance?"

"Dance?" Conrad said. "I dare say, I forgot all about it. How's the planning going, young man?"

Billy turned to him, looking disgusted. "My ma has been working on her dress and talking about it non-stop. She's about to drive my pa plumb loco."

Wallis smiled. "And why is that?"

"On account she tells him he has to dance with her." Billy shook his head in dismay. "I hope I don't have to dance with anyone. What a sight that would be."

Wallis and his brothers laughed. "Billy, when you're a little older you won't mind dancing with a pretty girl."

Billy stuck his tongue out. "Yecch! Girls."

Wallis laughed again. He wished he felt the same way right now. Unfortunately, he didn't. Jean was driving *him* plumb loco. The thought of going to the dance with her was both exciting and terrifying. He could well imagine what it would be like to spin her around the grassy dance floor, which caused a chill to run through his body.

He tried to work, but his mind kept returning to thoughts of dancing with Jean. If this kept up, he'd be worthless the rest of the day. Thankfully Jean hadn't returned yet. She must be helping Dora with the dishes. But when she came back, he'd have to do his best to avoid her. Attraction was one thing, dealing with powerful feelings another. He didn't want them and had better stay busy, or his attraction might get the better of him.

When Jean showed up, she wasn't alone. Letty was with her. "Oh, my," Letty whispered as she stepped into the library. "This is wonderful!" She went to the nearest shelves and ran her fingers along the spines. "And look at all the books that were donated."

"I know," Jean said with a cheerful smile. "I can't wait to get more."

"Leave yourself some shelf space," Sterling advised as

he approached. He went straight to Letty and kissed her on the cheek. "Nice, isn't it?"

"It's just what this town needs." Letty smiled back. "I hope you don't mind, but I'm stealing Jean for a time."

"What?" Wallis said as he approached. "What are you doing?"

"We're supposed to be having a dance Saturday, remember?" Jean said.

Wallis stiffened. "That soon?"

She nodded. "Have you forgotten?"

"Actually, Billy just reminded us," Conrad said. "Poor Oliver. I do hope he'll be able to attend."

"This means we'll have to borrow Mr. Smythe's horse and mower," Irving said. "We'll want the grass short if we're going to use that area for dancing." He looked at Conrad. "We're still using the meadow behind the captain's saloon?"

Conrad nodded. "Right you are."

Wallis glanced at Jean again, and images of dancing with her returned. He wanted to escort her to the dance, but quickly shoved the idea from his mind. That was a road he just couldn't go down. He forced a smile. "Well, I better get back to work."

Jean nodded, also smiling weakly. "I know."

Wallis turned back to his half-finished shelves. Jean and Letty left and he sighed. He had to stay away from her, or else the attraction between them was going to ruin everything. He didn't want to stay here. Wallis also didn't want Phileas staying. His older brother had to take over the estate, the title, deal with their mother …

"I guess I better go too," Billy said. "My ma has chores for me to do and she's going to pay me." He gave Wallis and his brothers a pointed look. "A worker is worthy of his wages, don't you think?"

Conrad chuckled. "And how much do you think you're worth, young man?"

Billy scratched the back of his head. "At least ten cents an hour."

"You strike a hard bargain, Mr. Watson," Conrad bent to him. "Very well, ten cents it is. Are we in agreement, chaps?"

"I don't mind paying it," Wallis said. He also wouldn't mind following Jean and Letty, but that wasn't the wisest thing right now. He focused on Billy. "So, are you going to get all gussied up for the dance?"

Billy scrunched up his face. "What for? I ain't gonna dance. If I did that, I'd have to touch a girl! Yecch!" He ran for the door and went outside.

"In about ten years that boy's going to change his mind," Sterling commented.

"Is Letty getting excited for the dance?" Wallis asked no one in particular.

Sterling put a hand on his shoulder and gave it a shake. "She certainly is. She's been working on a new dress. All the women have, as far as I know."

"Jean hasn't," Wallis heard himself say.

"Why not?"

He looked at Irving. "I don't think she has money to buy the fabric. Nor does she have the time, what with working on the library. What about Sarah?"

"I plan on buying her dress for the dance." Irving slapped Wallis on the back, then headed for the door. "In fact, I'm going across the street to take care of that right now."

Wallis casually followed him. "Are you talking about one of those ready-made dresses?"

Irving laughed. "Well, I'm not sewing her one, now am I?" He opened the door and went outside.

Wallis caught up. "Which dress?"

Irving stopped and turned to him. "Why are you so interested?"

Wallis thought of the pretty pink dress with the tiny roses and embroidered collar. Jean would look lovely in it, and he hoped Irving didn't have that one in mind. "Just curious," he finally answered.

Irving nodded and started walking. "I believe I have just the dress in mind. Now let me see if I can find it ..." He trailed off as he reached Alma's store.

The bell on the door jingled as they stepped inside. Wallis took a quick look around, spied the rack of ready-made dresses, and glimpsed the pink one with the embroidered collar. It was still here.

Alma stepped out from the back with a smile. "Well, how can I help you two today?"

Irving looked around before spotting the dresses. "I'd like to get something for Sarah to wear to the dance." He headed for the rack. When he reached it, he pushed dresses aside trying to find the one he wanted. He stopped when he got to the pink dress. "I had another one in mind, but this isn't bad."

Alma beamed. "Ah, that would look beautiful on her. Shall I wrap it up for you?"

Irving cocked his head. "What if it doesn't fit?"

"Then bring it back and I'll refund your money. But we both know Sarah can alter it easily enough."

Irving looked it over as Wallis' heart sank. If he said something, it would give away that he was growing sweet on Jean. But wait a minute ... isn't that what he wanted? True, his original plan was to get Phileas to think he was. But to make it believable he'd have to do a few things, like escort Jean to the dance, hold her hand, look lovingly into her eyes and all that rot. It was bound to get him into trouble, but ...

"Then yes, please," he heard Irving say. "That would be very kind of you." He turned to Wallis. "Sarah's going to look beautiful in that dress."

Wallis hid his disappointment with a smile and did his best to match Irving's enthusiasm. "I'm sure she will." He wanted Jean to have a beautiful dress, one that he could admire her in from afar, because if he got too close, he was liable to lose his heart. Part of it anyway.

He looked at the remaining dresses on the rack and tried to convince himself that a ready-made dress would look too bulky and ill-fitting, then let out a breath he wasn't aware he'd been holding.

"Well, I'm done." Irving held up his package.

"So, I'll see you two at the dance?" Alma asked as they headed to the door.

"Yes, you will," Wallis replied, his heart sinking further. Dash it all. He felt cheated not getting Jean a dress.

He stepped outside with an odd twinge in his heart. Jean would go to the dance in her homespun dress, decent as it was, but not much to look at ... he shook his head. He was being ridiculous. It wasn't his problem. Jean was a big girl and could take care of herself.

He was about to turn away and head back to the library when his feet stopped. He spun around and faced Irving. "I'm going back inside."

"What for?"

"I need to ask Alma something. I'll see you in a few minutes."

Irving gave him a parting wave and headed across the street. Wallis watched him go then hurried back inside. "Alma, I want you to do something for me, but you can't breathe a word of it to anyone."

Her eyes lit up. "What did you have in mind?"

"Promise me, not a word to a single soul." If Wallis could drill holes into her brain with a look, he'd be doing it now. Maybe he was.

"Sure." She took a step back. "What is it?"

"I want you to pick out a dress for Jean for the dance. Deliver it to her home, and if she asks who it's from, tell her ... well, don't tell her anything. Someone wanted her to have a dress for the dance – that's all she needs to know."

Alma grinned ear to ear. "Mr. Darling, it would be my pleasure."

The next day the Darling brothers returned to Sarah's house to paint and fix a few more things. Wallis left a note on the library door that he would be by that afternoon to take another look at her place and get started if he could.

Jean sighed as she set the note aside. She should sort through and catalogue the remaining books and leave him alone to do what he needed to do. The last couple of days had been magical, yet terrifying. Her heart was ready to meet Wallis Darling head on, the rest of her wasn't. Or maybe it was the other way around. She wasn't sure at this point.

She brought a stack of books to the small desk in the corner and created a catalogue card for each. Some books she'd read, many she hadn't, and thought to take a few home. Then she'd have something to occupy her evening hours.

When Wallis arrived that afternoon, it surprised him how much she'd done. "The library looks wonderful, Jean. You must be very proud."

"What about you? You did a lot."

He smiled. "And my brothers, who are still at Sarah's. She and the children are helping paint the house."

She smiled. "They are? How many colors?"

He nodded as he chuckled. "Five, if Lacey has her way. She thinks each outer wall should be a different color, along with the porch posts." He strolled to the center shelves. "When will you seek more donations?"

She shrugged. "I'm not sure."

"You could make an announcement at the dance." He turned to her with a smile. "Or I could."

"You? But the library's not your responsibility." She pulled a book off a shelf. "Though I appreciate the offer."

He smiled, then gave her a quick list of the work he wanted to complete for her that afternoon. "It's going to take me about three or four days to get everything done."

"If you're working alone?"

"Yes. Phileas is taking a last look at the hotel to see what he'll need. He's eager to get started."

She nodded solemnly. "So, your plan for us is moot."

He smiled. "I suppose so. But Phileas ... well, I don't think I have to worry too much."

He didn't sound very convincing. Had he come up with something else to make sure his brother returned to England with him? "Are you sure?"

He ran his finger over the top of some books. "Phileas and Dora are friends, nothing more." He swallowed hard, and she knew he was trying to convince himself.

"Dora doesn't trust easily. I doubt she'd allow herself to get sweet on your brother."

"Yes, but that's what the rest of my brothers and I thought about Sterling, and look what happened." He crossed the library to the desk. "We still need to get more chairs."

She surveyed the interior and couldn't believe her eyes. Wallis and his brothers had worked wonders. "I can pay you."

"For what?"

She waved a hand at their surroundings. "This. You did an incredible job."

"Keep your money. Seeing the look of satisfaction on your face is payment enough. My brothers will agree." He leaned against the desk. "Oliver wished he could have helped."

Jean smiled. "Poor Oliver. He's missing out on a lot of things the last few days."

"Including talk of the dance," he said. "I meant to tell him last night that it's only days away."

Jean took a deep breath. She didn't want to think about the dance and didn't have the time or funds to sew a dress. She'd have to wear her Sunday best and hope it was good enough. Jean sighed, sensed Wallis watching her, and looked at him. He was staring. "What is it?"

Wallis shook his head. "Nothing. It's just, for a few seconds, you looked ... happy and sad mixed together. Makes me wonder what it must have been like for you and the others. Losing loved ones."

135

Jean swallowed hard and nodded. "It wasn't easy. I miss my pa every day. The loneliness can be unbearable. Hope and prayer help." She smiled at him. "That and human kindness."

Wallis blushed as he came away from the desk. "I hope you're coming to the dance. You deserve to have some fun."

Jean smiled. "Thank you. I might just do that."

Wallis grinned and nodded. "Good, it's settled. I'll leave you to your work. I have your floorboards to tackle."

She nodded and smiled. Although their conversations reminded her she wanted to be loved and love in return, she'd take things slow and enjoy each moment as it passed. She knew Wallis was a decent man, and even though the odds weren't in favor of him staying simply because he'd grown sweet on her, she was still hopeful their paths might cross again in the future. She smiled to herself as she thought of the possibilities.

As she showed Wallis out, her heart skipped a beat. Yes, she was attracted to him, but he'd also grown on her. As she closed the door and looked back at her new library, she knew Wallis Darling was proving to be more than just her handyman. He was becoming a friend.

She got back to work, organizing and making a list of titles she'd still like to have. She'd just finished when Alma came in, a package tucked under her arm. "Wow! Look at this place!" She came to the desk and set the package down. "I can't believe so much work was done already." She went to the nearest shelf of books. "Can I check one out?"

"Certainly." Jean beamed. "Any book you like. I'll make you a card." She grabbed an index card and scribbled down Alma's name.

"Am I your first customer?"

"No, Billy Watson has that honor."

Alma laughed. "Why am I not surprised?" She looked the shelves over. "So, um, do you have any romance novels?"

Jean blushed. There were a few she wouldn't mind reading and had no idea where they came from. She didn't pay attention to titles and authors while she and Billy were collecting donations. Jean smiled at the thought then noticed the package. "What's that?"

"Oh, yes." Alma brushed some of her red hair out of face. "This is for you."

Her eyes widened. "What?"

Alma smiled. "Yes. It's a gift."

"From whom?"

She shrugged. "I was given instructions to deliver it to you."

Jean didn't know what to think. "What is it?"

Alma bit her lip as she smiled. "Open it and see."

She picked up the package, tore off the string and unwrapped it. "Oh ... my ..."

"Pretty, isn't it?"

Jean held up the dress. It was the purple one with the lace trim. She ran her fingers over the delicate material and gasped. "It's gorgeous." She looked at Alma, her eyes misting. "It must be from Wallis."

Alma shrugged again. "Maybe someone saw you through the store window looking at dresses and decided to surprise you with one."

Jean smiled, her hands trembling. It must be from Wallis. He was so thoughtful and his gift touched her. "I don't know what to say." She suddenly froze. "It's not from you, is it?"

"No, of course not." Alma gasped. "Not that I wouldn't get you a gift, but only for your birthday or Christmas. You know me."

"Yes, I know how you like to give people gifts on their birthday. But it's not my birthday."

Alma gave her a heartfelt look. "No, it's not. Besides, you don't have to say anything about the dress to anybody. Just go to the dance and enjoy yourself."

Jean smiled as a warmth she'd never experienced before washed over her. Wallis had made her feel special, even though he wasn't staying in Apple Blossom. She couldn't help but wonder if it was more than friendship growing between them. What if he really was sweet on her? The thought was strange but exciting all the same. No one had ever been sweet on her before.

She admired the dress. Whatever happened between her and Wallis, she knew one thing for certain – she'd never forget his kindness. "Oh, Alma. What would have become of us if the Darlings hadn't come to Apple Blossom?"

Alma set the book she had on the desk. "To be honest, I don't know. More might have left, and some wouldn't have made it through winter. Look at Sarah and her children. I was getting worried about them, but then Irving came along and they fell in love."

"Letty too, and Cassie."

"And you?"

Jean laughed. "No. Not me." She stared at the floor. "Wallis, Oliver and Phileas will return to England." Her heart sank at the thought, and she tried to ignore it by concentrating on the dress in her hands. "I should try this on."

"Come to the store and I'll put on some tea. You can try it on while the kettle's heating."

Jean smiled, folded the dress, then they left the library. She'd make a few nice memories with Wallis Darling and have one lovely dress to help her remember him. She didn't have the right to ask for more.

Chapter Eleven

Wallis left the library and headed for the hotel. He'd enlist Oliver's help, seeing as how Jean wouldn't be home for a time. He hoped his brother didn't leave behind the smell of skunk when they left, but he'd get done quicker with an extra pair of hands.

He entered the hotel, didn't see anyone, and went upstairs. He knocked on Oliver's door and waited. No answer. "Ollie?"

Silence.

"Where could he be?" He returned downstairs and went into the kitchen. "Dora, have you seen Oliver?"

"He's taking another bath." She smiled.

Wallis sighed. "Poor chap."

"He's determined to go to the dance." She picked up the coffeepot. "Want some?"

"Don't mind if I do." He sat at the table and waited for her to serve him.

"When is Phileas coming back?" She poured him a cup. "And did you finish at Sarah's?"

"We gave the house a fresh coat of paint. White with green trim. To the despair of Lacey, who wanted us to paint it pink, purple, green, and yellow."

She cringed. "Oh, my."

"Indeed." He smiled and took a sip of coffee. "That's good. Thank you."

She returned the pot to the stove. "So are you looking forward to the dance?"

He tried to hide his smile. "I am. A dance is always fun and invigorating. Though I'm afraid my brothers and I might not be familiar with your country dances."

"They can't be that different."

"You'd be surprised. But no matter, I'm sure we'll pick them up in no time. Oliver especially – he loves to dance. So does Phileas."

Her head snapped round to him, then she glanced away. "Is that so?"

Wallis winced. Was that interest in her eyes? "Yes. He's light on his feet."

She smiled as her cheeks pinked. "He's snuck into the kitchen a few times without my hearing him."

"Has he?" He smiled but said nothing more. He didn't want to encourage a conversation about his brother, unless it involved their leaving Apple Blossom. He was having a hard enough time battling his growing feelings for Jean. But the call to return home was stronger. For now.

"So, how's the library looking today?" Dora poured herself a cup.

"Good. Jean is happy. The work suits her well." He took another sip and smiled at the memory of Jean's face lit up with happiness. The library would keep her busy. Now if she could make a decent living, he'd rest easier. But the library would not see her through rough winters, especially not if Agnes had her way. He'd have to speak to Irving and Sarah and see what their plans for the old millinery shop were. Nothing was settled yet, and probably wouldn't be until after they married.

In the meantime, there was the problem of Rev. Arnold leaving. He should speak to the Arnolds or the captain and find out what was going on with that. Sterling mentioned having the captain keep a lookout for a new preacher in Bozeman, but how long would that take? Captain Stanley could put an advertisement in the newspaper there, he supposed ...

"You look lost in thought," Dora commented.

"I was thinking about the Arnolds."

"Oh, yes." She sighed and set her cup in its saucer. "I heard the captain took them to Bozeman."

"What?!"

She nodded. "I thought you knew."

Wallis gaped at her. "We didn't think he wasn't leaving until after the dance."

She shook her head. "His health is failing, Wallis. The

sooner the captain gets him to Bozeman and a doctor, the better. They left early this morning."

"How did you find out?"

"I saw them head out. Mrs. Arnold must have urged the captain to take them late last night. I know it means the weddings will have to wait, but that's okay. It gives Cassie, Letty and Sarah more time to work on their dresses."

He sat back in his chair, eyes wide. "No preacher."

"I know. I have no idea what we'll do come Sunday. Mr. Watson might hold a Bible study for the town. He's done it before when Rev. Arnold was too sick to preach."

He stared at the table. "I'd better tell the others." He drained his cup and stood. "Thank you for the coffee, Dora." He put on his hat, tipped it, and left. He'd run upstairs and tell Oliver, then head to Sarah's to tell the others. Who else in town knew?

And what about the weddings? Sure, Letty, Cassie and Sarah had more time to make their dresses, but it could take weeks, maybe months to get another preacher. What then? Would Sterling, Conrad, and Irving return to England with him and the others? If so, they could still come back to Apple Blossom to wed their brides. And what of Phileas and Dora – would this development turn his head away? Did he dare hope?

He went upstairs to the bathroom, but Oliver wasn't in it. He must be in his room.

When he knocked on the door this time, his brother answered. "Wallis, what are you doing here?"

"I've come for you. I need help with Jean's place." He stepped inside. "Did you know that Captain Stanley took the Arnolds to Bozeman this morning?"

Oliver's jaw dropped. "What?!"

"Yes, that was my reaction." Wallis went to the bed and sat. "I'm not looking forward to telling Sterling or the others."

Oliver sat in a chair on the other side of the room. "I can just imagine the look on our brothers' faces. How will they marry?"

"I don't know, short of going to Bozeman or Virginia City." Dash it all, the idea was sound enough that Sterling and the others might do it. Maybe he should get to work on Jean's place and let Dora be the bearer of bad news. "Can you help me with some things at Jean's place?"

"Of course, anything." He lifted an arm and sniffed. "I'm better today."

Wallis left the bed and took a few cautious steps toward him. "Hmm, you're right."

Oliver beamed. "Maybe I can dance and not make anyone pass out."

He laughed. "Let us hope." He thought of Jean, the dress he'd purchased, and smiled. "Get your socks and boots on, then let's go."

Oliver hurried to comply. As soon as he was done, they left and went to Jean's. "What does her place need?"

Wallis tried his best not to grimace. "A lot, but thankfully, there's not much space to work on. As you can see, it's quite small."

"I *do* see." Oliver went to the door and opened it. "She doesn't keep it locked?"

"Who would steal a coffin?" Wallis stepped inside. "There are some floorboards that need to be replaced. Thank goodness it isn't the entire floor."

Oliver nodded as he looked around. "What's in there?" He pointed at the door to the storeroom.

"Again, not much." Wallis opened it so his brother could peek inside.

"Right, storage."

He closed the door. "And Jean's bedroom at one time." He sighed and looked around the larger room. "When her parents were alive. She lost her mother years ago, then her father when ..."

"Yes," Oliver interjected. "I know."

Wallis nodded. There was no more to say on the matter.

They got to work, tearing up the bad floorboards, then went to the feed store to buy some new ones. Once they got them in, they went to Alma's to see what paint she had. They'd bought a lot for Sarah's house, so white and green were likely out of stock. "What about yellow?" Oliver asked as they stepped inside the general store.

"We'll see what she has." Wallis went to the counter but there was no sign of Alma. "Where could she be?" He rang the bell on the counter. "Alma?"

They heard someone coming down a set of stairs.

Alma popped through a door leading to the back and smiled. "Hello. I was upstairs having another cup of tea. You just missed Jean."

Wallis' face grew hot. "Oh?"

She smiled as her eyes flicked to Oliver. "Yes, she tried on a dress someone gave her as a gift."

Oliver smiled. "How nice."

"It's for the dance." She gave Wallis a look.

He cleared his throat then pointed at some paint cans stacked in a corner. "Got any yellow?"

"Sure do. I still have some white too. Is this for Jean's place?"

"Yes." He went to the paint and examined the cans. "I see you have red. I'll take some of that too."

"Red?" Oliver said. "What for?"

"She needs a new sign. We need to make her one."

"Yellow with white trim and red lettering?" Alma said.

"Yes." Wallis smiled at Oliver. "You can handle the sign – you've got a steadier hand than I."

"Sure." Oliver looked around the store before giving Alma a lopsided smile. "Am I terrible?"

She leaned toward him and sniffed. "It's still there, but better than it was, I imagine."

"You have no idea," Wallis said. "We'll take three cans of the yellow, one white and one red."

"Will we need that much red?" Oliver mused.

"What we don't use, Phileas will." Wallis began carrying cans to the counter. He skipped over any conversation about Jean's dress. Oliver didn't need to know he bought it and he wasn't about to ask Alma how it looked on Jean. He'd done enough imagining on his own – it kept him up half the night.

Back in the library, Jean ran a hand over her new dress. She was positive Wallis had to have bought it for her. This made her pleased and anxious at the same time. It meant nothing, of course, other than he wanted her to have something nice to wear at the dance. Yet a part of her wanted it to be more, which was silly. He was leaving. The man was being kind, that's all. Goodness, after seeing her place, he probably pitied her. She wasn't sure what to think about that.

Alma gave her a hanger for the dress and Jean hung it up in the window behind the desk. She didn't want to wrinkle it by keeping it folded. When she took it home, she'd hang it somewhere and then Wallis would see it. Would he comment? Cast brief glances at her? Maybe his cheeks or ears would turn pink. Who knew? But she was looking forward to finding out.

She finished her cataloguing and debated gathering more book donations. But the pull to head home was too great, and she finally gave in. She carefully folded the dress, tucked it under her arm and locked up the library. Thank goodness the frock fit and wouldn't have to be altered. She was a decent seamstress but nothing like

Sarah or Cassie. Half the time, she took things to Cassie to mend or hem.

When she arrived home, she heard hammering coming from inside the tiny building, and she smiled. Should she sneak past Wallis, go upstairs and display the dress properly? It sounded like fun.

She peeked through the door's glass panes and caught sight of Wallis and, to her surprise, Oliver. She slipped inside as Wallis went into the storeroom, his brother following.

She tiptoed past the storeroom door and flew up the staircase quiet as a mouse. Once inside her living quarters she giggled, then hung the dress on a nail Pa pounded into the wall for his coat next to the bedroom door. When Jean stepped back to admire it, her smile grew wider as she remembered how the dress looked on her. It was truly a work of art. She fingered the lace trim and pondered heating the iron, but as long as the frock remained on its hanger, it should be okay.

She jumped when she heard someone coming up the stairs and darted over to a chair. Her heart thudded like a drum when she heard Wallis' voice coming from the stairwell outside. He must have been talking to Oliver because she could make out both voices.

Then their conversation ended, and Wallis knocked on her door. "Jean," he called out gently, "are you in there?"

She giggled and hesitated before responding. "Yes, I'm here."

Wallis opened the door and peeked inside with a kind smile. "I thought I heard you come up here and wanted to say hello." He stepped into the room, his eyes gravitating to the dress. He stared at it a moment, jaw slack. "It's beautiful."

Jean beamed at him as admiration rippled through her like electricity. For a moment, their eyes met and time came to a stop. She couldn't breathe and there was only him. What was happening?

Wallis broke the spell with a chuckle. "I'm sorry, I didn't mean to barge in. I should go downstairs and get back to work. Oliver is waiting." He took one last look at the dress before he turned to the door.

"Don't go," she blurted. "I ... I can make you some coffee or tea. Oliver too."

He gazed at the dress again, smiling warmly. "You're going to look lovely in that."

A giddy tremor went through her. "Funny thing about that dress. Alma delivered it to me and said an anonymous person wanted me to have it."

He stepped toward her with a slow nod. "I see. But ... how could he be anonymous if he bought it from Alma?"

She shrugged. "I don't know. Maybe he left some money and a note."

He walked over to the dress and ran a hand down the bodice. "Well, he has good taste. This is beautiful."

She swallowed hard, catching his mistake. "What makes you think a man bought this for me?"

149

His cheeks flushed a bright red as he coughed and stepped away from the dress. "Uh, I didn't mean to imply that."

Jean smiled as butterflies filled her belly. "That's okay."

Wallis cleared his throat, obviously relieved she wasn't saying it was him. He gestured to the door. "Anyway, I should return downstairs and get to work."

Jean nodded and headed into her tiny kitchen. "I can still make that coffee."

"Thank you," he said, eyes on the dress again. "That would be lovely."

A flutter of warmth went through her at the sight of him admiring the dress. It reminded her of how comfortable things had become between them since they'd started working on the library.

Oliver appeared in the doorway. "What's going on?"

She smiled at him. "I'm making the two of you some coffee."

"Oh, jolly good." He looked around, his eyes coming to the dress. "Wow, did you make that?"

Jean blushed head to toe and looked at Wallis. "No, it was a gift."

Wallis coughed a few times then grabbed some cups and saucers from her little cupboard and set them on the counter. "Tell us when the coffee's ready and we'll come up and have some."

Jean nodded as she busied herself at the stove. Poor Wallis must be grateful she hadn't pressed him further about the "mystery" of who got her the dress. She kept smiling to herself and thinking of the dress until she poured two cups of steaming black coffee, then called Oliver and Wallis back up to her rooms.

The men sat down at her kitchen table and each took an offered cup. There was an awkward silence for a moment before Wallis surveyed the table. "Cream and sugar?"

She smiled and fetched the cream and sugar bowls. By now his ears were bright pink again. She couldn't remember when she'd had so much fun.

The three talked for a time, touching on topics from literature (naturally) to Rev. Arnold, and of course the dance. Wallis mentioned he and his brothers had a lot of work between now and then but would help set things up.

Jean felt her cheeks flush as she hid behind her cup, sipping whenever she smiled. She didn't want to give away that she knew what Wallis had done. She didn't know if Oliver noticed their silent exchange. He was probably too worried about the skunk odor still clinging to his skin. She could smell it now that he was sitting across from her and doubted a few days would make much difference. Not unless he bathed well every day until the dance. Poor man, few would want to dance with him smelling the way he did now. But there was nothing anyone could do about it.

"Thank you for the coffee," Wallis announced as he stood. "Oliver and I must get back at it."

"We bought paint," Oliver announced happily. "We're going to paint the building yellow."

"With white trim," Wallis added with a smile. "And we'll make you a new sign."

"Red paint for that." Oliver grinned. "I'm making it."

She closed her eyes a moment. The dress had distracted her from the important work they were doing. "Thank you," she said when she opened them. "From the bottom of my heart."

Wallis smiled again. "No one should have to live in something that makes them uncomfortable. To have a roof over one's head, four walls and a hearth, well, why not make them the best you can? We'll paint the outside, then work in here."

"Yellow," she stated. "With white trim and," she looked at Oliver. "Let me guess, a white sign with red letters?"

"Of course." He grinned again then stood. "I say, but the place will look downright cheery by the time we're done with it."

Wallis crossed his arms and smiled at her.

Jean rolled her eyes. "All right, I concede. Cheery."

Oliver glanced between them. "Am I missing something?"

"I told her I wanted this place to be cheery, not some gloomy, dark building that looked like death belonged there."

"Or something to that effect," she said. "Even though this *is* a funeral parlor."

Oliver smiled. "Cheery it is, then." He headed for the door. "Thank you for the coffee, Jean." He went downstairs.

Wallis gazed into her eyes and smiled again. "Thank you."

She returned his gaze. "Thank you."

His face flushed red again before, with a parting smile, he left the room.

Jean bit her lip and grinned like a loon. "He knows I know." And she planned to have some fun with that.

Chapter Twelve

"He did what?!"

Wallis absorbed Sterling's shock. He decided Dora shouldn't have to be the one to tell his brothers, so he did. "Can you blame him?"

Sterling sat back in his chair, his mouth half open. "No, of course not. If the reverend's health is failing, he needs help immediately." He glanced at Letty, who'd joined them for dinner. "I'm sorry, darling."

She shrugged and smiled. "It's all right. This gives me more time to work on a dress."

He nodded, his eyes going to Irving and Conrad. Cassie, Sarah, and her children were also in attendance. "Right," Conrad said. "Well, we wait, I guess."

"Or travel to Bozeman," Oliver said from his table in the corner.

Wallis cringed. He would have to say that.

Letty put her hand over Sterling's. "We'll talk about it later. We have the dance to worry about."

"Yes," Phileas said. "Why not discuss something more cheerful? For all we know, Captain Stanley will return with a preacher."

Everyone nodded in agreement and got back to eating. Wallis glanced at Jean, who sat across the table from him. She began whispering to Cassie, who smiled and giggled. He didn't know what they were talking about but enjoyed seeing her happy. But Jean's eyes didn't hold the same happiness Cassie's did. The three brides glowed with it. Especially Sarah, who kept giving Irving loving glances.

Wallis' heart pinched, and he fixed his eyes on his plate. Love hadn't stabbed him yet, and he had to make sure it didn't. He would go home, live out his life in England, perhaps get himself a nice cottage in the country, far away from his meddling mother ...

"When can you get the mower from Mr. Smythe?" Dora asked no one in particular.

"I'll speak to him tomorrow," Sterling said. "I meant to do it earlier, but we painted the exterior of Sarah's house."

"Thank you," Sarah said. "It's going to be beautiful. I hate leaving it now."

"Don't say that, Ma," her son Flint said. "Our new place is huge, and I get my own room."

"Don't worry, Flint," Irving said. "You'll still get to

live in the bigger place. But until your mother and I are married, you'll have to stay in your current home."

Everyone was quiet for a moment as Wallis poked at his salad and looked around. Conrad could still act as Cassie's deputy but would have to remain in the hotel for now. Same with Irving, though nothing was stopping him from working on the old millinery shop. Hmm, time for a few questions. "So, what are your plans for Flint's new room?" he asked Irving. "For the whole building, for that matter?"

"We're not sure yet," Sarah said with a smile.

"I still think Sarah and Jean should do something together," Irving said.

Jean looked up from her plate. "What?" Her eyes flicked to Irving and back. "What do you mean, do something?"

Sarah shrugged. "Sewing, baking, making things to sell. Who knows?"

"Baking what?" Jean asked.

"All sorts of things," Irving said. "Pies, cakes, cookies. The town could use a bakery. Think of the time you'll save the other women. They can come get their baked goods from you instead of having to make things themselves."

"And we could offer a mending service, maybe even make a few dresses," Sarah added.

"Nothing sells better than convenience," Sterling commented. "If people can buy time to do the things they'd rather be doing, trust me, they will pay for it."

Wallis watched Jean with interest. "It would supplement the library," he said.

She nodded. "You're right, it would." She smiled at Sarah. "We'll talk about this later. Thank you for thinking of me."

"I'd be a customer," Dora said. "If I could get baked goods from you, that would save me all sorts of time."

"See what I mean?" Sterling cut up his roast beef and took a bite. "Delicious. Dora," he said and waved a fork at her. "Don't stop making this."

A smile spread across her face as she turned to Sarah. "You've got yourself a customer."

Sarah smiled at Jean. "Sterling's right. Together we could handle a bakery and at least some mending."

"But what about your laundry service?" she asked.

"It's my hope Sarah gives that up altogether," Irving said. "Sewing and baking will be enough. Besides, if no one has to bake they'll have time to do their own laundry."

Everyone laughed and discussed the possibilities that could come of the plan. Since it was getting late, the women decided to meet the following morning to work out the details.

Wallis sighed in relief by the time dessert was served. If Jean began working with Sarah, and could scrape some income from library donations, she'd make it fine.

"You look happy," she commented across the table.

"Do I?" he said with a smile. "I would think you'd be

the one that's happy. This solves some things for you, doesn't it?"

She nodded with a knowing smile. "Thank you."

He gave her a wink and sipped his coffee. Now he could rest easy knowing she was taken care of and enjoy working on her place. He still wanted to talk her into renting or buying Sarah's old house – it was the perfect size. She could rent her old lodgings over the funeral parlor to a young bachelor or sell him the business altogether. The job wasn't fit for a woman in his opinion.

He watched Jean through dessert and, when it came time for her to leave, offered to walk her home. "You don't have to," she said. "It's just across the street."

"An evening stroll, then," he suggested.

She smiled. "Very well."

Outside the hotel, the light of the setting sun cast long shadows on the street. Wallis offered his arm, and to his surprise, Jean blushed. "So formal," she said.

"A gentleman always offers his arm to a lady. Is there anything wrong with that?"

She smiled, shaking her head. "Not at all. It's just that you never see it around here, not even among the married couples."

The two walked, a comfortable silence between them. The streets were quiet, the only sound the thump of their shoes as they moved along the boardwalk. They stopped at the library and watched the Featherstones drive by in their buggy. Agnes gaped at them, but Wallis didn't care. He could feel the warmth of Jean's arm in his, and it made his heart beat faster.

The air was a little humid, but the warmth was pleasant. With the sun setting, the purple sky was fading to navy blue. It was a beautiful sight and, without thinking, he pulled Jean onto the library's bench with him. They sat in silence a few moments, content in each other's company, and stared across the street at the funeral parlor. Wallis wondered if he should say something but decided against it. This was nice, peaceful, serene. Part of him wished it could go on forever.

Flint and Lacey came out to play and chased a ball down the street. Conrad and Cassie left the hotel, and he noticed Cassie was on Conrad's arm as they headed to her place.

"We should go," he announced.

She gave him a contented smile. "Fine."

When they arrived at Jean's door, Wallis paused for a moment, unsure if he should say goodbye. He was enjoying this too much.

Jean faced him, smiling. "Thank you for walking me home."

He smiled back. The urge to kiss her was overwhelming. Great Scott, where did that come from? He took a step back. "It was my pleasure," he said huskily.

She seemed to sense his hesitation and smiled at him knowingly. "I'll, um, see you tomorrow." She nodded in farewell and opened her door, slipping inside before he could say anything else.

Wallis watched her go with a pang of regret in his chest. He stood there for a moment longer before turning away, not sure what had just happened or what it meant. But he knew one thing—he wasn't ready to let Jean go just yet.

❧

The next day in Alma's, Sarah and Jean ran into each other and started a brief discussion about the bakery/mending service. They would meet at the hotel later for lunch with Dora and talk about it, but Jean had thought about it most of the night and was getting excited.

But that's not all that was exciting in Apple Blossom. Their conversation turned into making final plans for the dance on Saturday. Mrs. Watson and Mrs. Atkins got in on the conversation. Cassie and Letty came into the store and joined in along with several other women shopping in town. As Alma's store was no place to hold a decent meeting, the group walked to the church for the seating. It was strange not seeing Mrs. Arnold flitting about, and Jean wondered if the town would ever see the Arnolds again.

Julia Brighton showed up with her daughter Jandy. "Alma said there was a meeting. How come no one told me?"

Cassie smiled. "This was impromptu. Everyone's been so busy with other things that we haven't had one until now. Don't worry, whatever we discuss we'll pass on to others."

"Well, that makes sense." Clara sat in a pew with her daughter and glanced around. "Where's Agnes?"

"Don't say that too loud," Jean said. "She's liable to show up."

Clara sank a little in her pew and nodded. Everyone knew if Agnes was there, she'd take the meeting over and try to have everything her way.

"All right," Dora said. "Let's get started."

Mrs. Lewis raised her hand. "What are we going to do about a preacher?"

Cassie sighed. "This is about refreshments and decorations for the dance, Anna, not a new preacher. Besides, the captain is going to check into some things while he's in Bozeman."

"You're leaving the hiring of a new preacher in the hands of that buffoon?!" Everyone cringed as Agnes marched down the church aisle. "What's going on? Why are you all gathered? You have no business here!"

Jean exchanged a look with Cassie and Sarah. Letty was at her ranch.

Mrs. Tate stood. "Agnes, we threw this together at the last minute while some of us were discussing the dance in Alma's store. The church doubles as a meeting house so we're using it."

"You didn't ask me," she snapped.

"You weren't in the store," Cassie pointed out. "And

as you can see, there are others that are not in attendance."

Agnes looked around. "Then thank heavens I showed up when I did. Who knows what a mockery you'd make of the refreshments and decorations."

Jean sighed and sank in her pew. "Here we go," she whispered to Sarah.

She nodded in agreement and rolled her eyes at Cassie.

As Cassie stood before everyone, she couldn't make a face or roll her eyes. Instead, she had to watch Agnes storm the rest of the way to the front of the church and turn to the lot of them.

"We don't need a lot of decorations. What a waste of time."

The women all exchanged the same look of angst. "Agnes, it's not up to you how many decorations we have," Jean said.

Agnes tossed her hand in the air. "Well," she huffed, "I'm not putting any up. When do I have time for that? Forget it."

"No one said you had to," Mrs. Tate pointed out.

"Good, because I'm not," Agnes snapped back. "What about the food? Have you organized it yet? Don't go getting too fancy. No one wants to be cooking all day."

Sarah pinched the bridge of her nose. "Some of us don't mind."

"Well, then you're an idiot."

Jean stood. "Agnes, why are *you* here? No one's asking you to do anything. If you don't want to, that's fine, but don't tell the rest of us what to do."

Agnes went red as her eyes narrowed. "Someone has to make sure this doesn't get out of hand. Before you know it, someone's spiked the punch and a brawl will break out."

Now *everyone* rolled their eyes. Agnes was just being Agnes, but it could drive the sanest person around the bend.

"Why don't you let us handle this," Cassie suggested. "Then you won't have to worry about any of it."

Agnes looked her up and down. "Is your betrothed still at the hotel? You haven't moved him in yet, have you?"

Cassie's jaw dropped. "How dare you!"

Agnes looked smug. "There's no preacher. That idiot captain isn't bringing one home. That means no marrying." She looked at Sarah. "And you, I take it you're still living in that shack of yours?" She looked over the little crowd. "The last thing we want in this town is more ungodliness."

Jean got to her feet. "Agnes, do you want to help plan the dance or not?"

"No," she said with a wave of her hand. "I'm not wasting my time." With that, she stomped down the aisle and out the door.

Jean let out the breath she was holding as the church doors closed.

Mrs. Tate stood and slowly clapped her hands. Mrs. Watson was next, followed by the rest of the women.

Jean blushed to her toes and shrugged. "Someone had to do it."

"Thank goodness you did," Sarah said. "That woman is going to drive me loco."

"She's already done it to me," Cassie said. "If I could arrest her, I would. A few days in jail might do her some good."

Mrs. Brighton shook her head in dismay. "I can't imagine being so unhappy."

"Unhappy?" Jean wondered.

"Yes, dear," Mrs. Brighton said. "Why else would she be so awful all the time?"

"Some people just are," Cassie said. "They're mean, spiteful, wicked, and ignorant. Every town has a person like that or close to it. We have Agnes."

Everyone looked at the church doors. "So what do we do about it?" Jean asked.

"There's nothing you can do," Cassie said. "Agnes and Mr. Featherstone own the only bank in town." She sighed, then faced everyone again. "All right, who wants to be on the refreshment committee?"

Several hands shot up. Cassie took a head count then went to the podium and wrote their names down. "And the decorations?"

The rest of the hands went up. She wrote their names too. "Mrs. Tate, do you want to be in charge of the refreshment committee?"

"I'd love to. Ladies, if you'll come here, we'll make some plans."

Jean watched as Dora, Mrs. Watson, and Mrs. Lewis went to join Mrs. Tate, and followed. She was better at cooking than decorating. The rest joined Cassie in the front pews.

They came up with a list of main dishes and desserts, and another list of some of the remaining women in town. They'd ask if they'd like to be on a committee and what they'd be willing to contribute. With only four days until the dance, they'd have to speak to the other women today. "Jean, since you have a horse, can you ride out to Letty's, the Atkins' and the Smythes' and let them know about the committees?" Mrs. Tate asked. "Find out who would like to do what?"

She smiled. "Of course, I can go right now if you'd like."

"That would be helpful." Mrs. Tate wrote something next to Jean's name. "And you'll bake a cake?"

"Yes." Jean smiled at Dora. "I can use your oven?"

"You know you can." Dora stood. "I'd better make a list of what we'll need and get to Alma's."

Everyone chatted about the upcoming dance and Jean noticed Cassie and Sarah were especially excited. But of course, they had someone to dance the evening away with.

She thought of Wallis and wondered how many times he'd dance with her. Would the Darlings think the town's little gathering silly? From the sounds of it, the brothers had attended grand balls back in England. Apple Blossom's dance was in a mowed meadow lit by torchlight. They had a handful of musicians, food prepared by local women, and decorations made of whatever they could find. Hardly the stuff of grandeur.

"I should go." Jean left the pew and headed for the church doors. Outside she followed the lane that led to Apple Blossom's main street, stopping in front of the parsonage. The Arnolds had occupied the two-story house for as long as she could remember. Its yellow paint was peeling, the white trim no better.

Out of curiosity, she went up the porch steps and tried the door. It was unlocked. She stepped inside and saw that some of the furniture was gone. Would Mrs. Arnold have the captain retrieve the rest and deliver it to them in Bozeman?

She went to the staircase by the door and ran a hand along the rail. She knew the house had two bedrooms upstairs and a small one downstairs. The parlor was a decent size and so was the dining room. She'd hadn't seen the Arnolds' kitchen in ages and headed for it. The dining room table and half the chairs were also gone, and the china cabinet in the corner was empty. In the kitchen, the table and chairs were still there, along with a large hutch and the stove. There was even a small icebox.

Jean went to the backdoor and looked at the yard. There was no fence between the parsonage and the church. She wondered if the new preacher would have a family. If so, the house would suit them fine. She smiled at the thought and left.

She stopped at home on her way to the livery stable and found Wallis and Oliver fixing the window in her storeroom. "What are you doing?"

Oliver looked sheepish. "I'm sorry, but my hammer slipped out of my hand and I broke your window."

Her hands went to her mouth as she took in the damage. Thank goodness he'd only broken one pane. "Oh, dear." She mustered up a smile for Oliver. "It was an accident."

"Yes, but that doesn't mean I don't feel terrible about it."

"We'll get some glass and fix this," Wallis said. "You've nothing to worry about."

"Speaking of ... um, fixing," she hedged. "The parsonage could use some work."

The brothers exchanged a look of surprise.

"You don't have to do anything. But, should you have any leftover paint, as you know, it's yellow with white trim."

Wallis sighed, then smiled. "And you'd like to see it fixed up before a new pastor arrives, is that it?"

"If we're going to do that," Oliver said, "why not look at the doctor's house, too?"

She smiled at Wallis. "Could you?"

He sighed as his hands went to his hips. "It means more time."

Her heart leaped. "Yes, I know."

Wallis looked into her eyes and stepped toward her. "Oliver, Phileas and I have only so much."

She looked at the floor. "I know that too."

"No worries," Oliver said. "You'll still have Sterling, Conrad and Irving here to help."

Jean swallowed hard as she looked at Wallis. "Yes." She forced a smile. "I'll speak to one of them." Her heart in her throat, she left to saddle her horse.

Chapter Thirteen

Wallis watched Jean go, sensing her disappointment. He turned to Oliver, who was oblivious to their silent exchange. His brother had finished measuring the windowpane and was jotting the measurements down. As soon as he did, Wallis nodded at the door. "Why don't you go see what Alma has in stock?"

Oliver studied him. "You okay?"

Wallis nodded, his heart pounding. Jean didn't want Sterling, Conrad or Irving to work on the parsonage. She wanted him to do it. She wanted him to stay.

Wallis grabbed the top crate of a stack to steady himself. *He* was attracted to her and had growing feelings. Now he realized she did too.

"Wallis?"

"I'm fine," he said and waved Oliver away. "See to the glass."

Oliver nodded and left the storeroom.

Wallis wasn't far behind. "I have to talk to Jean. I'll see you later."

His brother nodded. "Sure." He headed down the boardwalk to the general store while Wallis started for the livery stable.

Inside he found Jean saddling Mr. Brown. "Need any help?"

She looked at him over the horse's back. "No, thank you." She ran a brush over Mr. Brown's back a few times. "What are you doing here?"

"Oliver's checking on the glass. I thought I'd see if you needed anything?"

She smiled nervously. "Like what?"

He looked at the horse. "Like saddling Mr. Brown. I could accompany you."

"On a ride?"

"Sure, I have a horse."

She shrugged. "Suit yourself. I'm off to Letty's, then the Atkins' and Smythes'. I need to tell them about the dance committees and what we've decided."

"Which was?" He headed for his horse. Sylvester was three stalls down.

"I'm on the refreshment committee. I need to see what committee the other women want to join, then tell them who to talk to. The sooner we get to work on things for the dance, the better."

He led Sylvester out of his stall and tied him to a post

next to Mr. Brown. Jean handed him the brush. He set it aside and followed her into the tack room. Before she could get to her saddle and blanket, he had them and was already on his way back to her horse.

"Do you have to be such a gentleman all the time?"

He put Mr. Brown's blanket on first. "Of course. If not, my mother will go into a fury the likes of which the world has never seen. People may get hurt ... *will* get hurt. It would be ugly."

She leaned against a post and watched him. "Somehow I doubt that."

He put the saddle on next. "My dear woman, you have never met my mother."

"Will I?"

He froze and stared at her over Mr. Brown's back. "That all depends."

"On what?"

He cinched the saddle. "You know what. Sterling, Conrad, and Irving."

"Do you think your parents will come to visit Apple Blossom? Or insist your brothers, should they remain, come with their American wives and visit her?"

"She'd prefer the latter, but we don't always get what we want. I can see Sterling balking." He sighed. "He's balking now."

"What harm is there if he stays?" she asked.

He checked the saddle then headed for the tack room. "Like I said, you don't know my mother." Wallis wondered if Sterling had written to their parents. Part of him doubted it. He'd wait until after he married Letty. Then Mother would have to accept her.

He returned with Sylvester's bridle. Jean was putting Mr. Brown's bridle on him. "I miss my mother," she whispered.

Wallis snapped to attention. "I'm sorry she's gone. Sorry about your father too."

She managed another weak smile. "I thought I could handle being alone. And I have so far. I have friends."

"Of course you do." He watched her a moment, unsure of what she was trying to say. He gasped when he realized what it could be. "Cassie, Letty, and Sarah?"

She shrugged. "Sarah and I know each other, but she's not as good a friend as Cassie and Letty."

"I see. And now all three are getting married to my brothers."

She looked him in the eyes. "Yes."

His heart went out to her. "Jean, this is a small town, therefore it's easy to make friends. You have Alma …"

Her eyes widened.

"Okay, so she talks your ear off. But she's … kind."

Jean nodded. "She is. And as alone as I am."

He went around the horses to stand before her. "Jean, you needn't feel all alone. You're not losing friends to marriage. You're making new ones. My brothers are fine chaps and will help you with whatever …" He looked into her eyes. By Jove, was that longing he saw? "Um, they'll be happy to help you with whatever you might need." He swallowed hard. If he didn't move, he might kiss her. What a disaster that would be. All his plans to return to England ...

"I'm sorry," she said. "I don't mean to burden you."

He watched her a moment, unsure what to say. He was still trying to put himself in her position. What if he was the only one to return to England? What a horrid thought.

She led Mr. Brown to the stable entrance and went outside. She mounted as Wallis led Sylvester out. Once he was on his horse, they set off down the road. It was a warm day, and he enjoyed the sweet smell of apples surrounding them. He and his brothers hadn't helped pick this week, but as the captain had gone to Bozeman, there was no one to take them to Virginia City. Had he taken a batch to Bozeman to sell?

They were quiet the first half mile as they headed for Letty's place first, by way of Sarah's house in case she was helping Sterling paint. Sure enough, that's where they found her and the rest of his brothers. "What brings you here?" Sterling asked as they dismounted.

"I need to speak to Letty." Jean went through the gate and around to the back of the house.

Sterling, hands on hips, watched her go and turned to Wallis. "She looks determined."

"She's delivering news about the dance. The women have formed committees and are trying to get things organized. Saturday is only four days away."

"I'm looking forward to it." Sterling looked skyward.

"It will be nice dancing beneath the stars, and there'll be a full moon."

Wallis smiled. "It will make for a romantic evening." He sighed.

Sterling eyed him. "What's wrong, brother?"

Wallis met his gaze. "I don't know. I'm ... not myself."

Sterling half-smiled and looked at the house. "Why are you accompanying Jean?"

He shrugged. "I ... offered to tag along."

Sterling gave him a knowing look. "I see."

Wallis' eyes rounded. "It's nothing like that."

"Isn't it?"

He took off his hat and ran a hand through his hair. "Not at all."

His brother smiled. "Mm-hmm."

"Really."

Sterling shook his head with a smile. "Whatever you say, Wallis."

Good grief, did it show? Was his attraction to Jean that obvious? Or was it he was spending time with her when he could work on her place? "I needed an outing."

Sterling smiled at him, then turned on his heel and headed for the others. Wallis followed, looking at the house as he went. When they reached the others, he spied Lacey painting a board green and smiled. "What is she doing?"

"She has to paint something," Irving said. "I'll use it for the chicken coop."

Flint came running out of the house. "Jean, where's my ma?"

"Still in town," Jean called back. "Working on the dance."

"Oh." The boy sat on the back porch steps.

Jean went back to speaking with Letty as Wallis distracted himself studying the house. "It looks good," he said to no one in particular.

"Yes," Irving agreed. "Have you spoken to Jean about it?"

"Of course, but she didn't think it was something she could afford. But if she's working with Sarah, it's feasible."

Irving put a hand on Wallis' shoulder. "Would she mind living out here?"

"I don't know. She misses her parents and is already feeling lonely because her friends are marrying."

Irving gave his shoulder a squeeze. "Poor Jean. Such a thing never occurred to me."

"How could it? Our minds have been on fixing things before returning home." He looked Irving in the eyes. "You're staying."

"I've said as much."

Wallis swallowed hard and nodded. Like Jean, he was losing people close to him to marriage. He had to take his own advice and see this differently. He was gaining sisters, new friends that would become part of his family. But they were all staying here as far as he knew, so he shared the same lonely feeling Jean had. He didn't like it but what could he do?

"Come look at Sarah's bedroom," Irving said. "We've moved the furniture back in."

Wallis forced a smile and followed his brother to the back door. His eyes gravitated to Jean before he went inside, and once again his heart went out to her. What would happen if he acted on his feelings? No one said he had to stay. Maybe Jean would like to live in a cottage in the English countryside. Hmm, it was something to think about. But did he dare?

Jean rode alongside Wallis as they headed for the Smythe farm. He was quiet and contemplative. What could he be thinking? She watched the road and tried not to guess. Her throat was thick with emotion. The realization that he was leaving had hit, and she didn't want him to. Merciful heavens, when did this happen? She was attracted to him – that was no secret, at least to herself. But this went far beyond attraction, and she'd thought she had a handle on her heart. She was wrong.

She swallowed hard and tried not to look at him. Every time she did, she felt a pang of longing. She told herself she wouldn't let her heart have its way, and somehow it did. The sneaky thing was pounding right now. Every time she glimpsed him out of the corner of her eye, it leaped in her chest, accompanied by a pain she didn't know. Was her heart breaking? But the only thing to cause that would be ... *oh, no.*

She glanced at Wallis. How did she fall in love? She couldn't have. Feelings toward him might have grown over the last few days, but love? She didn't believe it. She missed her parents, that was all. That coupled with losing her friends to marriage had made a big fat hole in her heart. Wallis filled it, that's all.

Tears stung her eyes at the thought of his leaving. What would fill the hole once he was gone? Would they write to each other? Would he come back to visit his brothers? What if the Darling brothers that stayed behind packed up and went to England as soon as they wed? It could happen.

Jean thought of Dora and tried to take solace in her still being here. She hoped. She'd been and would be, spending a lot of time with Phileas. He was charming, handsome, and loved the hotel almost as much as Dora did, and he hadn't so much as lifted a finger yet to fix things. She closed her eyes at the thought.

"Jean, are you all right?" Wallis asked gently.

She opened her eyes, looked at him and sighed. "I'm fine."

"Are you?"

She stared at the road ahead. "No." She brought Mr. Brown to a stop. "I'm ... " She didn't know what to say.

"Sad?"

She saw the concern in his eyes and her heart melted. "Yes."

"About my brothers marrying your friends."

She nodded.

He sighed and dismounted.

"What are you doing?"

He went to the left side of her horse. "Come on, then, get down."

"What? Why?"

"Just do it."

She didn't know what was going on but dismounted anyway. "Now what?"

Wallis looked into her eyes, pulled her into his arms, and held her. "I know it hurts ..."

Did he have to say that? The threatening tears escaped in full force. "Oh, Wallis, what will I do without them?" Without thinking, she cried into his chest. "I don't want them to leave."

"And I don't want my brothers to stay." He held her tighter.

Jean thought she might faint. His embrace was firm, safe and comforting. She didn't want the hug to end. "I'm s-s-sorry. I don't mean to c-cry."

"It's all right, darling. You cry all you want. Sometimes a good cry does wonders."

She laughed. "How would you know?"

He drew back enough to look at her and smiled. "So I've heard."

"From your mother?"

"Oh, heavens, no. My mother makes Napoleon look like a bawling baby. No, I ... know people who've told me."

"Women?"

"Yes."

She sniffed back tears. "Well, seems we have the same problem."

He stepped back, his hands on her arms, and rubbed them a few times. "We do. But we mustn't let it get the best of us." He smiled. "Now, chin up. We'll get through this together."

Part of her was relieved, while the rest only knew he was leaving. "How?"

"We're friends, aren't we?"

She nodded.

"We can get through the dance, then after I'm gone, write to each other. You'll tell me how my brothers are doing, won't you?"

Fresh tears fell. "I will." So he still wanted to leave. That was that.

He tucked a finger under her chin and brought her face up to his. "There, there, let's have no more tears. After all, I'm trusting you to look after everyone for me."

Her heart broke. "Oh, Wallis ..." She turned away, mounted her horse and headed down the road.

He mounted Sylvester and followed. "Jean, wait." His horse trotted to catch up. When he came alongside her, he gave her a heartfelt smile. "I'm sorry, did I say something to upset you?"

"It's nothing." She swallowed hard. For a moment or two, she thought he was more than a little sweet on her. But she must have read him wrong. Besides, she'd never been in love or been sweet on anyone before. Nor had she ever had someone sweet on her. What were the signs? They gazed into each other's eyes a few times, his voice became soft and husky now and then, but ...

"Jean?"

"Wallis, I said it was nothing."

He faced forward. "I'm sorry, I don't mean to press."

"It's all right. You tried to comfort me, and I thank you."

He nodded. "You're welcome."

They rode in silence until they reached the Smythes. Mrs. Smythe invited them in for coffee. Wallis went to find her husband and speak to him about borrowing either Sally or Walter and his sickle mower to create the dance area for Saturday. Jean sipped coffee with Mrs. Smythe, talked about the dance and the dresses some of the other women were making, and told her about her own.

She left out the part about Wallis having bought it for her. There was no sense letting people know. They'd think there was something between them, and though Wallis had talked her into pretending there was to distract Phileas from Dora, their little charade somehow fizzled. Problem was, she had feelings for him, but it was one-sided. If it wasn't, he'd *do* something, wouldn't he? Tell her how he felt, want to spend more time with her? Kiss her?

Okay, he was here with her now while poor Oliver was stuck replacing part of her window in the storeroom ...

She pushed the thought aside as she sipped her coffee and chatted with Mrs. Smythe about whatever popped into her head, if only to distract herself. The pain in her heart was real, which made her feelings for Wallis real. They hit with such force; it surprised her she could mount her horse earlier. If only he hadn't held her in his arms like that, she'd be okay. But he had, and she wanted more. What was she supposed to do now? Should she even go to the dance? Would it make the pain worse to spend more time with him?

"What's the matter, dear?" Mrs. Smythe asked as she poured her a second cup of coffee.

"Nothing, ma'am."

The older woman sat. "If I didn't know any better, I'd say you have the look of a young woman with a broken heart. Whatever is the matter?"

Jean met Mrs. Smythe's concerned gaze. "Everything."

She put a hand over one of Jean's. "My dear sweet child. You don't have to tell me unless you want to. But know this, whatever it is, this too shall pass." She glanced out the kitchen window. "It's that young Englishman, isn't it?"

Jean gasped.

Mrs. Smythe gave her a knowing look. "Oh, dear, you've fallen in love, haven't you?"

She took a shuddering breath. "It shows that much?"

"I wore the same look myself, many years ago." She gave her hand a pat. "When I fell in love with Chester. He was so handsome – still is, mind. But I almost lost him to another. I was shy, you see. I almost lost him to Loretta Fiddlebottom."

Jean snorted. "Fiddlebottom?"

"That was her name. A catty thing, she was. Black hair, dark eyes, wicked tongue. She knew how to flirt and could wrap a man around her finger in no time at all. Including my Chester. That is, until I got the nerve to speak up."

Jean smiled. "What happened?"

"I told Chester how I felt about him. I figured it was worth the risk. The most he could do was say he didn't feel the same, then I figured Loretta could have him. But I wasn't that cruel, which was another reason I had to speak up."

Jean stared at the checkered tablecloth. "What good would come of telling him? Wallis is leaving."

Mrs. Smythe smiled. "Because if you tell him, you won't have to live with the regret of knowing you didn't."

Jean wiped her eyes and nodded. "I suppose you're right." She smiled at her. "Thank you, Mrs. Smythe."

She smiled back. "Well, with your folks gone now,

you need someone older and wiser to talk to. I don't mind being that person."

Jean left her chair and hugged her. "Thank you."

Mrs. Smythe patted her on the back. "Anytime, child. Anytime."

Chapter Fourteen

"Would you like to return to town or wait for me?" Wallis asked.

Jean glanced at Mrs. Smythe and back. "I can wait."

Wallis smiled. "This won't take long. We just need to hitch Sally to the mower." He left the Smythes' kitchen and returned to the barn where Chester waited. "She'll wait," he announced, then went to Sally's stall. "Hello, girl."

Sally's ears pricked forward as she looked at him.

"She thinks you have a treat," Mr. Smythe explained.

"I'm afraid I don't." He patted Sally's neck. "After the work is done, I'll see what I can do."

"She loves her apples." Mr. Smythe opened the stall door and led Sally outside. They hitched her up and Mr. Smythe sat on the mower and got her going. "I'll see you there."

"We'll be right behind you." Wallis waved and headed back to the house. Jean looked sad, almost careworn when he'd entered the kitchen earlier. Had she been crying?

This time when he went in, she looked better. "I'm ready to go." She brushed cookie crumbs from her dress and left the kitchen table.

"Here." Mrs. Smythe held up a bag. "Some cookies for the road."

"Thank you." Wallis took it. "I'm sure I'll enjoy them."

"Best you enjoy them before you get back to town," Mrs. Smythe advised. "There's only a few and you have five brothers."

He laughed. "You're right, I'll eat them on the way back." He smiled at Jean. "I take it you've had some?"

"I have."

He studied her. Yes, she looked better, yet tired. "Come, let's get back to town."

They said their goodbyes, left the house and headed out. "Where's Mr. Smythe?" Jean asked.

"He had a head start. Don't worry, we'll catch up." Wallis took a cookie and munched on it. "Want one?"

"No, thank you. I had my share already." She rode alongside him and didn't so much as bat an eye in his direction. Hmm, had he done something, said anything? He didn't think so. Maybe she was still upset over the idea of losing her friends once they married. But at least those friends would still be in Apple Blossom. He didn't know when he'd see his brothers again after he returned to England.

They rode in silence for a time and Wallis tried not to think about Sterling, Conrad, and Irving in marital bliss. Once they got married, that is. Who knew when that would be now?

He stole a glance at Jean. She still sat stiff in the saddle, eyes on the road. "Do you think Oliver will dance?"

She glanced his way. "So long as his partner can stand the smell."

"What if we perfumed him up?"

"Perfumed?" She cringed. "That might be worse than the skunk smell."

"He can take it."

"Yes, but what about the rest of us?"

Wallis smiled. "Poor Oliver."

"His poor dance partners."

"You'll dance with him, won't you?"

She smiled. "Will you?"

He laughed. "Of course not."

"Coward."

Wallis laughed again. At least she was smiling now. "I'm sure he'll dance a quadrille at least. Do you know how?"

"Yes, most folks in town can. At least he'll be moving in circles and back and forth. Has he tried lemon again for the smell?"

"I believe so." He watched the road a moment as

Sylvester plodded along. He could see Mr. Smythe and Sally about fifty yards ahead, then watched them disappear around a bend in the road. "Are you making anything for the dance?"

"If you mean food, then yes. A cake."

Wallis smiled. He was making idle conversation, but wanted her talking so she wouldn't be alone with her thoughts, whatever they were. He didn't enjoy seeing her sad and was trying to figure out how to keep a smile on her face. "What kind?"

Jean looked at him. "Chocolate."

"Oh, my. I might faint."

She laughed. "I might want to see that."

He looked shocked. "You wouldn't."

"I would. I've never seen a man swoon before."

He chuckled. "Neither have I. But if I'm the one swooning, what good does that do me? I'll still not see it."

"But everyone at the dance could tell you about it." She gave him a sly smile. "We could even take a picture. The captain has a camera."

"Does he?" He shook his head. "Is there anything that man doesn't have?"

A blush crept into her cheeks. "I don't know. His saloon is full of all kinds of things from his travels. Books, charts, swords, guns, and things that none of us have ever seen before and have no idea what they are."

"How interesting." He was curious now. "We should

have tea with him when he returns and let him regale us with fantastic tales."

She smiled again. "My father used to tell me stories of adventure when I was small. Some terrified me while others had me so enthralled, I couldn't go to sleep. He always told me not to tell my mother."

Wallis laughed. "Great Scott, they *were* tall tales, weren't they?"

She shrugged. "I don't know. Half of them I've forgotten. The ones I can remember were in some books of fables and poems."

He looked at the road. "My mother used to read to us when we were very young. Sometimes Father would too. I often wonder if being read to when young makes a difference."

"Of course it does," she said. "Books are wonderful things. They take us places we could never go by ourselves. China, India, the deepest, darkest jungles of Africa."

"Speaking of Africa and India, will Billy be able to read the book he checked out?"

"Some of it, but he'll have to have his father read it to him. At least until the captain returns. Captain Stanley enjoys reading stories to the children. I don't know what we'd do without him."

"And now you've lost your preacher," he said.

She looked at him. "I don't know what we'll do about that either. No preacher, no teacher for the children, not to mention a schoolhouse."

He studied her a moment. Her features were etched with concern. "Now I understand why you asked us to help with the parsonage. You can't afford to lose another preacher."

"No one in town is a clergyman. Mr. Watson has taught a few times, but he doesn't want to do it full time. And he's not licensed."

"There is that."

She was quiet a few moments, but he caught her glancing at him now and then. She looked ... hurt. Confused. And dare he say, a little angry. But why? What had Jean and Mrs. Smythe been talking about?

When they reached town, they went straight to the meadow behind the saloon. Conrad and Cassie were there. Good, Wallis wanted to double-check the size of the dance area. They'd have to mow enough to cover the seating and food tables.

Conrad waved at them. "You read my mind, brother!"

Wallis smiled and waved back. Mr. Smythe was already walking toward Conrad. He noted he'd left Sally and the mower where he thought the mowing might start. The two were speaking by the time Wallis and Jean reached them.

Jean dismounted and headed for Cassie, putting on a smile for the town sheriff. Was she in a better mood, or trying to put on a pleasant face? Either way, something was bothering her, and he didn't think it had to do with her friends getting married.

189

For now, Wallis didn't have time to think about it. He'd let Mr. Smythe ride Sylvester home. When he finished mowing, he'd take the mower and Sally back to the Smythes' little farm then ride his own horse on his return trip to town. Maybe by then Jean would tell him what was wrong, even if he had to ask.

Jean stood next to Cassie and watched Wallis prepare the mower, then get in the seat. Mr. Smythe stood to one side and gave instructions as Conrad looked on. Soon Sally was plodding along, the mower doing its work and clearing the area for a dance floor.

"This is going to be fun," Cassie said. "A dance is just what this town needs."

Jean nodded, unsure what to say. Mrs. Smythe's words still echoed in her mind. *Tell him* ... But how could she tell Wallis she was falling in love with him? Would he laugh at her, tell her she was being silly, or stare her in the face and say, "I'm sorry if anything I've done or said has misled you ..."

Jean fought against a sigh as Cassie told her the decorating ideas some women had come up with. She listened, nodding at appropriate times, but her heart wasn't in it. She was too busy thinking about what Wallis would say if she told him how she felt. Jean wanted so badly for him to stay, and maybe he would if she told him about her growing feelings. But the fear of rejection was fierce. Maybe it would be easier to deal with a broken heart.

The mower continued its work, cutting a wide swath through the grass. Jean watched Wallis guide Sally in a large rectangle and felt a wave of admiration wash over her. He was so handsome and confident, she couldn't help but feel drawn to him.

Cassie's voice pulled her back to reality. Jean forced a smile as she responded to her friend's questions. They chatted a while longer before she told Cassie she needed to unsaddle Mr. Brown, then get some work done at the library. As much as she'd love to stay and watch Wallis work, it would only make her sadder than she already was.

Jean glanced at Wallis once more and saw him looking at her with a concern that made her heart skip. Could he ... could he know what was going through her mind?

She hurried to the livery stable without looking back, too embarrassed by the possibility that Wallis might have figured out how she truly felt about him. But mercy sakes, the man wasn't some mind reader. Now she was just being silly, not to mention fearful. If she wasn't careful, that same fear would ruin what little time she had left with him. She needed to be brave, tell him how she felt – even if he rejected her – so at least they could still be friends when it came time for him to leave for England.

After unsaddling Mr. Brown and giving him a treat, Jean made a beeline for the library. Maybe she could get lost in some books and find a few stories to touch her heart or make her laugh out loud.

As she searched for new books to read, her thoughts strayed back to Wallis and their conversations together. His dry wit always caught her off guard and made her smile, but it was his kindness toward those less fortunate than himself that filled her heart with admiration. He was cheerful and saw good in everyone no matter what their circumstances or past mistakes might be – an honorable trait that few possessed.

Jean picked up a book, read the title, then set it aside. She picked up another, doing the same thing. Six books later she realized why she was so drawn to Wallis: he reminded her of someone else who made an impact on Apple Blossom with simple acts of kindness: her father! No wonder Wallis stirred up such feelings inside her.

"Oh, Pa, I wish you could have met him," she lamented aloud. "He's so much like you. Maybe that's why I've been missing you so much." She wiped a few tears away, then looked at the book in her other hand. After reading the title, she set it aside and picked up another.

She chose books for moments like these when Wallis filled her head more than any fictional character ever could. Because sure enough, the idea of telling him how she felt began creeping forward again. If by some miracle Wallis was here to stay, she wanted nothing more than to show him how much she cared for him. Now she just had to find the courage to do it.

Jean made a stack of books to help her forget things, then went to the livery stable, a book tucked firmly under her arm. The smell of hay and the soft nicker horses were things she liked about the stable. She sometimes sat on a bale and read. Jean would read, then try to think up what to say to Wallis. She was determined to talk to him about how she felt – even if it made her nervous as a cat in a room full of rocking chairs. Given enough time to rehearse what she wanted to say, maybe she wouldn't be so fearful of his response.

To her surprise, Wallis was in the stable when she arrived, looking over Mr. Brown's saddle with a critical eye. "Why didn't you put this in the tack room?"

"I ... forgot." Good grief, she was so wrapped up in having to talk to him, she'd left her saddle out. "Um, what are you doing here?"

Wallis smiled. "I came to get a treat for Sally. Conrad already fed her a couple of apples, but I wanted to give her a handful of grain or something."

"You two are going to spoil Mr. Smythe's horse." She clutched the book to her chest.

He nodded at it. "What have you got there?"

She blushed, set the book on a bale of hay, and took a deep breath. It was now or never. "Forget about the book, Wallis ... I've been wanting to talk to you about something."

Before she could continue, Wallis interrupted her, looking apologetic. "Will this take long? I've got to take

Sally back to Mr. Smythe's. Conrad is bringing Sylvester now."

Jean forced a smile and nodded in understanding. She couldn't be quick about this. It didn't seem right. After all, she didn't want to just blurt something out. "That's alright," she said softly. Jean gathered up her book and headed out of the stable.

"Wait," he called.

She did, closed her eyes and waited. The ache in her heart was getting worse.

He put a hand on her shoulder and gently turned her around. "Whatever it is you wanted to talk about, we can do so after dinner."

She had a sudden image of his brothers, along with Dora, Letty, and Cassie, listening in. "Um, perhaps."

"Is it all that important?"

She looked into his eyes. "I guess it depends on how you look at it." She nodded. "After dinner. Fine." She walked away, her throat thick with emotion. If she told him, and he told her he had no feelings for her, then what was she to do? How awkward would it be to converse with him in the following days? And what about the dance? Would he tell his brothers? Good grief, she might never look them in the eyes again.

She went across the street to the library, sat on the bench out front, and opened the book. It was a collection of adventure stories she hadn't noticed before. Maybe someone came by the library while she was at the Smythes' farm and dropped it off. Who knows what other books were brought in? She must have left the door unlocked.

Conrad led Sally, still hitched to the mower, to the livery stable and Wallis came out, some grain in his hands. He fed it to the horse, then waved at her.

Jean waved back as the men walked Sally down the road and out of town. Wallis might as well be walking out of her life, the way her heart was sinking to her toes. Maybe she wasn't as brave as she thought she was.

Chapter Fifteen

"Jean seems out of sorts," Conrad commented as they left town. "Is she?"

Wallis glanced over his shoulder at her. She still sat on the library's bench, her nose in a book. "Yes. But ... I'm not sure I should share what's bothering her."

"Can I help?" Conrad offered.

Wallis smiled. "Not really. In fact, you're part of the problem."

"What?" Conrad sighed. "What did I do this time?"

Wallis laughed. "Well ..." He scratched his jaw. He needed to shave. "You're getting married."

Conrad's face screwed up. "And that's a problem?"

"It is if you're taking away one of Jean's friends." Wallis gave him a somber look. "Jean feels she's going to lose all her friends."

"Nonsense," Conrad snapped. "She's gaining me."

Wallis smiled. "I tried to explain that, brother, but she's not as fond of you as the rest of us."

Conrad smiled. "I suppose I am an acquired taste."

"That you are. But I understand how she feels. I dare say, I can scarce think of leaving any of you behind." He looked back at Jean, still sitting on the bench. "Ah, Jean," he murmured. "You will always have your friends, no matter what life throws our way." The words seemed inadequate, but they were all he had at the moment. He wasn't sure who he was trying to comfort more, himself or Conrad.

His brother must have sensed the change in his mood. He sighed heavily. "Wallis," he said, "I didn't mean to upset her. None of us did."

"I know," Wallis answered softly. "She'll come around, eventually. At least Cassie and the others will still be here." He paused, thinking of his own life in flux and how his brothers' decisions to marry affected everyone in the group. It was a hard reality to face but one that no one could escape. What none of them had taken into consideration was how it would affect Apple Blossom. Their minds were on England. He mustered up a reassuring smile. "Everyone will be alright in the end," he promised.

Conrad nodded slowly before exhaling. "Life is an adventure, isn't it? Who'd have thought we'd wind up in a place like this?"

"You know what?" Wallis said, feeling lighter again. "I think life will always be an adventure when shared among friends who truly care for each other. I need to convince Jean of that. Perhaps then she'll feel better about the whole thing." He glanced past Sally at Conrad. "She wanted to speak with me. I told her I couldn't as we had to return Sally. What if that was a mistake? What if she had something crucial to say to me?"

"Then she'd have said it," Conrad pointed out.

"Hmm, I suppose." He remained quiet for a time, enjoying the peaceful afternoon, the warm sunshine and birdsong. Yes, life was an adventure, but it was also a journey, and where it led them was unknown. But that didn't mean they had to enjoy it any less. He had to make Jean understand that. He didn't want her to look at his brothers' marriages to her friends as bad. She could have adventures with the lot of them. Conrad alone could keep the town entertained for months on end.

When they reached the Smythes', Chester was waiting for them by the barn. "How did she do?" he asked.

Conrad patted the horse on the neck. "She's got a great sense of direction. The mowed area is almost a perfect rectangle. She got sidetracked by an apple on the ground, I'm afraid, but other than that she did fine."

Wallis chuckled. "She kept looking at it when I was driving."

"When I took over, she succumbed." Conrad patted her again and smiled at Mr. Smythe. "Thank you so much for letting us borrow Sally and the mower."

"Anytime, boys. I must admit I'm looking forward to

this shindig. The wife and I haven't danced in a long time."

"I say you make it an annual event," Wallis suggested. "I know there's talk of it."

Mrs. Smythe came out of the house and headed their way. "How did it go?"

Wallis noticed she had a small sack in her hand and wondered if it was more cookies. "Fine. I dare say, I don't think Sally needs us. She could mow that meadow all by herself."

Mr. Smythe laughed. "That she could."

Mrs. Smythe offered Wallis the bag. "For the ride home."

He smiled. "Thank you."

She looked around. "Jean didn't come with you?"

"I'm afraid not," he said. "When we left town, she was reading outside the library. There's nothing quite like having your nose in a book while everyone else is working."

Everyone laughed before Mrs. Smythe looked at the road. "She's lonely, that one." She looked Wallis in the eyes. "Her heart's just bursting to give love to someone. Mind yourself around her."

Conrad's eyes grew wide as he looked at Wallis. "What's this?"

Wallis coughed a few times. "Oh, nothing."

Mrs. Smythe shook her head. "Not to Jean."

His face fell. "What do you mean?"

She gave him a heartfelt look. "Young man, you've got eyes, haven't you?"

He shrugged and looked helplessly at Conrad. Not that he'd get any help from him. "I'm afraid I don't understand."

"Wallis," she said. "I'm only going to tell you this once. Be careful of a young woman's heart. Especially one who's never been in love before." She smiled again, eyes bright, then headed back to the house.

Mr. Smythe chuckled. "Wise woman, my wife. You'd do well to listen to her."

Wallis stared after Mrs. Smythe. "What ... did she just tell me?"

Conrad smiled and smacked him on the back. "Wallis, I think you'd better have that talk with Jean."

"But she's the one that wanted to talk to *me*."

Conrad shook his shoulder. "And when she does, pay attention. She might talk about one thing and mean another."

"You mean the way you are right now?" Good grief, he wasn't making sense of this.

"I think what Mrs. Smythe was trying to say is that Jean is sweet on you."

Wallis blanched. Though part of him hoped she was, it wasn't what he wanted to hear. It meant he'd have to hurt her. He was leaving, and if his guess was right, she was going to tell him how she felt. But he could be wrong. "Oh, dear."

"Indeed," Conrad said. "We'd best get back. Where's your horse?"

"I'll get him," Mr. Smythe headed into the barn. When he returned, they settled Sylvester, helped him unhitch Sally and put the sickle mower away.

"Thank you ever so much, sir," Wallis said as he mounted his horse.

Conrad mounted up behind him and gave Mr. Smythe a wave. "We'll see you at the dance."

"If not before." The old man waved goodbye then headed for the house.

Wallis watched him go and steered Sylvester toward the road. What to do? If Jean was indeed sweet on him, then he was going to have to figure out what to tell her. Either way, he could already picture the disappointment on her face and didn't wonder if he hadn't seen it already.

"You're being awful quiet, brother," Conrad said behind him.

Wallis swallowed hard. "I've been warned."

"What do you mean?"

He leaned down and patted Sylvester's neck. "You heard Mrs. Smythe say I should mind myself with Jean."

Conrad didn't answer immediately, then said, "Well, you should. If a pretty girl like her has taken an interest in you, how will you respond?"

Wallis thought about it. He didn't want to encourage her feelings, nor did he want to hurt her. He'd have to tell her the truth and make her understand that, at least as of right now, nothing could come of it. England and home were what mattered. He had to stay the course. He sighed and looked at the winding road before them. "I'll need to be honest with her and let her know not to expect too much from me."

"I couldn't agree more," Conrad said. "If that's truly how you feel."

Wallis' heart clenched and his mind churned. He would do his best to make things right with Jean, and more than that, he prayed she would understand. This journey was uncertain, but it was also a journey he would face head-on.

"Wallis?"

"I'm thinking."

"I say," Conrad said. "You won't know how she feels unless you ask her. That might be the best way. You don't want to leave things unsaid."

Wallis sighed again. His brother was right, of course. He'd have to talk to her. It would be difficult, he knew, but it was the only way to move forward.

Conrad clapped him on the back. "Chin up, brother. You'll find a way."

Wallis nodded and steered Sylvester down the road. He hoped so. He also hoped Jean found her way in her new life, even if it didn't include him. Wallis wished her the best, no matter what. He just prayed she would find the happiness she deserved.

Wallis swallowed hard and hoped he wasn't about to take away what little happiness she had.

Jean paced in front of the little desk in the library. She would have gone home, but Oliver was still there, and she wanted to be alone. Not that she'd be alone for long here, but as the library wasn't officially open yet, she'd have a better chance.

"You should tell him." She stopped pacing and leaned against the desk. "Just ... get it over with."

She sighed. She was making this harder than it was. Still, fear was a hard master, and she was terrified of creating a situation where she'd be even more miserable than she already was. If Wallis didn't have any romantic feelings toward her, then she'd not only die of embarrassment, but wouldn't be able to avoid him.

Apple Blossom was small, and unless she wanted to cut herself off from her friends and hide in her hovel over the funeral parlor (at least until Wallis, Oliver and Phileas left), then she'd better be able to take the bull by the horns and tell him how she felt. Embarrassment was one thing, regret another.

But ... maybe there was another way. What if they did write to each other? Perhaps she could tell him after he was gone. Only problem was, there were no guarantees he'd be back. Then another thought hit, and not for the first time. What if Letty, Cassie, and Sarah all went to England? There would be no reason for any of the Darlings to return to Apple Blossom. She'd be completely alone.

Cold settled in her gut, and she hugged herself. It was an awful horrible feeling. She took a breath, then blew it out hoping to get rid of the chill. "Well, that didn't work." Jean started pacing again. She was getting herself worked up and for what?

Jean sat at the desk and looked at the stack of books on it. She still had to create catalog cards for them. She took another deep breath. "No one's going anywhere." She sighed in relief. Sarah still wanted to work out a few details, but they had a preliminary plan for starting a bakery. She'd be working with the woman almost daily, plus running the library. She'd be busy doing two things she loved. Surely that would sustain her heart for a time. She didn't have to have Wallis in the picture to be happy, did she?

Yet when she thought of him, her heart melted, she grew warm, and contentment settled over her. "Why did I have to fall in love?" It was a good question. But then, who wouldn't fall in love with one of the Darlings? They were handsome, smart, kind, generous, and of course cultured. Wallis was especially attractive as he shared many of her interests. She'd never find another man like him. Wasn't it worth the risk of rejection to speak with him? Besides, they could still be friends, couldn't they?

She put her hand over her heart. It ached at the thought of his leaving and she wondered if the pain would ever go away. The hole in her heart he started to fill, would empty again after he left and then what? She'd be miserable once more.

Jean stared at the desk. She *had* been miserable, hadn't she? Just like everyone else in Apple Blossom. If the Darlings hadn't come along, who knows what would have become of the little town. The Englishmen were breathing life back into it and even Agnes didn't put up as big a fuss over things.

But that didn't mean Agnes approved of the Darlings, only what she could get from them. Agnes was foremost someone who used other people for her benefit. If she couldn't use a person and their resources, they were nothing to her. Wallis and his brothers saw her true nature right away and steered clear. But when they had to deal with dear Agnes, they did it well.

She smiled at the thought. She'd have to speak with Mr. Featherstone again about the library, and make sure she could use some donations for her pay. Otherwise, she would run it for a while, but if the bakery took up too much time, she'd have to find someone else to take it over.

She busied herself with the small stack of books on the table and tried not to think about Wallis or his brothers. When she did, it hurt, and she wanted no more pain to deal with than she already had. Still, she was going to have to decide and either keep her feelings to herself or speak up. She'd never realized how cowardly she was until she fell in love.

Finished with the books, she took one from the stack, went out front to the bench, sat and read. She got through the first paragraph then rolled her eyes. She *would* grab the only romance novel in the stack. "Figures." She leafed through it anyway, looked at some illustrations, then set the book on the bench.

"Jean!"

She froze at the sound of Wallis' voice, took a deep breath and looked down the street. Wallis and Conrad were riding Sylvester to the livery stable. She smiled and waved, then snatched up the book. Maybe if she pretended to read, they'd leave her alone. If Wallis headed her way, part of her (the silly part that spit in the eyes of fear) would want to tell him how she felt while the other part (the one that, even now, wanted to bolt to the other side of town – make that Bozeman) had its reservations. She was still at war with herself and didn't want to be. But what to do?

Jean sighed, closed the book and went into the library. Maybe if he didn't see her when he left the stable, he'd think she'd gone home. She wondered if Oliver was still there or if he'd called it a day.

What she should do is see what ingredients she'd need to make her cake. The dance was Saturday, and there'd be no shortage of activity in town to get ready for it. Maybe she should have volunteered for the decorating committee too. Then she'd have lots to do between now and then.

The Darlings' original plan was to leave Apple Blossom after the dance. But not anymore. The new doctor wasn't here yet, and what about a preacher? She knew Wallis and his brothers wanted to make sure the doc wasn't some charlatan (even if he was Agnes' nephew) and might want to do the same with the preacher. But it might be months before they got one of those. And if Sterling, Conrad and Irving were here, they could handle that themselves. They didn't need the other three brothers.

She gulped. The only things holding Wallis here were the state of her two-room living quarters and Phileas' work on the hotel. There were a few others the Darlings had wanted to help. If she remembered right, Etta Whitehead the blacksmith was one. But would Sterling, Conrad or Irving offer to help her fix up the blacksmith's shop and living quarters in the back? Had any of the Darlings thought of this yet? "Oh, why does love have to be so ... so ..."

The door opened. Jean spun around to see Wallis step inside. "H-hello."

He smiled. "Hello, Jean."

She swallowed hard. "What are you doing here?"

"I came to ... well, you said you had something you wanted to talk to me about?" He looked at the floor. "I have something I want to talk to you about too."

A chill went up her spine. Suddenly she couldn't speak! Oh, drat and bother!

"Jean?"

She swallowed again, her throat dry. "Um ... you go first."

"Oh, I, er, was going to let you talk."

She stared at him, eyes wide, heart pounding in her

chest. *Say something!* She shook her head and backed into the desk. "I ... well, I wanted to say ..."

Before she could force another word out, Agnes entered the library. "Oh. What do we have here?" She closed the door and took in the shelves, books, and everything else. "How did you get all this done so fast?"

"With help, of course," Wallis said.

Agnes narrowed her eyes. "And I suppose you helped her?"

"Of course."

"Alone?"

Jean rolled her eyes. "Agnes, Wallis and his brothers put up the shelves for me."

Wallis nodded. "Even Billy Watson helped."

Agnes looked like she wasn't buying it. Her eyes narrowed further on Wallis. "And what are you doing here now?"

"I came to speak to Jean about something."

"He and Oliver are working on my place," Jean offered.

Agnes went to the nearest shelf and ran a finger across the spines, then looked at it, checking for dust. "At least the place is clean. See that you keep it that way." She looked around some more, then fixed on Wallis. "Well, say what you're going to say to her, then leave. Unless you're going to check out a book."

Wallis narrowed his own eyes. "Jean, I'll see you at dinner." He looked at her and smiled. "You are coming, aren't you?"

She nodded, unable to help it.

"Good." He turned and left.

She sighed in relief and leaned against the desk.

"Dinner? Where?" Agnes snapped.

"The hotel." She came away from the desk and cut across the library to Agnes. "Are you here for a book?"

"No, I came to see if this place had shaped up yet. You're further along than I thought you'd be." She looked Jean over, turned on her heel and left.

As soon as Agnes was gone, Jean pinched the bridge of her nose and tried to breathe evenly. The last thing she needed right now was Agnes looking over her shoulder and telling her what to do. It would drive her around the bend in no time.

Jean took a few deep breaths, squared her shoulders, then locked up the library. She should thank Agnes. She saved her from having to say anything to Wallis. But she still had to get through dinner, and after Wallis spoke what was on his mind, she'd have to say something or at least decide when to. After the dance, perhaps? After all, she didn't want to feel awkward around him on the most festive night Apple Blossom had seen in years.

Jean nodded to herself, smiled, then headed home.

Chapter Sixteen

Wallis returned to the livery stable and Conrad. His brother already had Sylvester settled in his stall and was tossing hay into it. "Thanks for taking care of him."

"No problem. Did you speak to Jean?"

"I never got the chance; Agnes came into the library."

Conrad winced. "Beastly woman."

Wallis nodded. "True, but this gives me more time to mull over what I want to say to Jean."

His brother nodded sagely as they left the livery stable. Conrad headed straight for the hotel while Wallis lagged, eyes fixed on the library. Was Jean still there or had she gone home?

He crossed the street to check. The door was locked. It was just as well. He wasn't looking forward to speaking with her. For one, his heart was balking, and he needed to get the thing under control lest he change his mind.

England and home *had* to come first. Maybe if Phileas saw his dedication to family and duty, he'd take the hint and not think so feverishly about redoing the hotel. They were running out of time. He left, knowing he'd see her at dinner. They'd talk then.

When he reached the hotel, he went upstairs to his room. He wouldn't mind a bath, so he headed for the kitchen to heat some water. Dora wouldn't mind if he helped himself to a couple of buckets and the kettle. So long as he didn't take up too much room on the stove.

When he entered, there was no sign of Dora, but he smelled something cooking in the oven. Roast chicken, perhaps? He helped himself to the large kettle, filled it out back, then did the same with the buckets. That done he returned upstairs and got some water running in the tub to add the hot water to. As soon as he had a decent amount, he shut the water off and realized his mind was a blank. Maybe that was a good thing. If he started thinking about Jean, who knows where his thoughts would take him?

That he was relieved not finding her in the library said a lot. Maybe he had more feelings for her than he thought. But he couldn't afford them. He had to return. Mother was going to be a bear to deal with and who knew what Father would do. When it came to handling the estate, their father was a force to be reckoned with. But anything having to do with marriage, well, Mother was like a yearlong winter storm you couldn't escape from. How was he going to explain Sterling, Conrad, and

Irving's desire to marry and stay behind in Apple Blossom?

Yes, they all had good reasons, but Mother wouldn't see things that way. She'd put up a horrible fuss no matter what, and he and his remaining unwed brothers would have to put up with it. And then ... she'd think about things; like how fast she could marry the rest of them off. He gulped at the thought.

But he also didn't want to have to run the estate. Phileas was better suited to it. Therefore, he'd take whatever their mother threw at them and know that he didn't abandon their father. Of course, there was the possibility he would take a ship to America and show up on Sterling and Letty's doorstep. He might even try to drag them back to England if it meant having Sterling take his rightful place when the time came. After all, he was the one Father groomed from day one to take everything over after he passed on.

Wallis went downstairs, checked the water, then hauled a couple of buckets upstairs. He dumped them into the tub and went to fetch the kettle.

Was he being a coward? Hmm, maybe. Was his freedom so important? Most definitely. Would Father entrust him to take over if things came to that? Yes, especially if there was time to teach him how to run the estate. But Wallis didn't want it.

Furthermore, Mother would parade him around in front of every marriage-minded mama with a decent daughter until she married him off. And it would be to a woman of her choosing, not his. The poor young lady wouldn't have much say either. Her family would have bagged a viscount. What luck! To the parents, he and the young lady were nothing more than pieces of real estate to be bought and sold. Or in this case, acquired. He shuddered just thinking about it.

As he soaked, he thought of Jean and all she'd accomplished this week. In a short time, she'd opened the library, got it going, and began talking with Sarah about opening and running a bakery. It was exciting for her, yet the sadness in her eyes was still there. Different now, but there. He knew part of it was from losing her father. But there was more to it, and he couldn't figure out what it was.

He stared at the ceiling and puzzled over their adventure in America. It had turned out quite different than expected. How much more so, the longer they stayed in Apple Blossom?

He dried off, dressed, tidied the bathroom and went to his room. A book he took from the library the other day was on his nightstand. He leafed through it, went to a chair, tried to read but couldn't. His thoughts kept shifting back to Jean. He was trying not to think of her yet could recall every detail of her face: her big warm brown eyes, her light brown hair, her creamy skin. He could barely contain his excitement at the thought of seeing her in the dress he'd purchased.

He was determined to make her feel special and yet wondered if his plans would backfire. What if she was, as

Mrs. Smythe said, sweet on him, and he hurt her? It might be better to speak to her in the days that followed the dance, rather than ruin her time at the event. He wanted everyone to have a wonderful time, including himself.

Wallis sighed, pushed his thoughts to the back of his mind, and tried to think of something else. It didn't work. He put the book down, went to the window and watched the clouds drift by. Until the dance, he had Jean's place to work on. But knowing that only made him restless and anxious about how everything would turn out.

He wanted things to be perfect for her, and not just her place and the library – the dance too, from the decorations to the food served. He knew she loved her new dress and wanted her to enjoy wearing it in a festive setting. She deserved a good time, especially after all the work she'd put into the library. And even if she wasn't sweet on him and they remained friends, there was still something nagging him in the back of his mind that he couldn't quite identify or push away. She ... needed something.

He sighed heavily and turned from the window. Instead of worrying about things he couldn't control, he should focus on what he could do – work on Jean's place and help her prepare for the dance. He wasn't sure what that would entail, but he'd try. Then he'd know he'd done all he could in advance to ensure that Jean had an enjoyable evening. Before he broke her heart.

He squeezed his eyes shut at the thought. "No, no, no. She might be a little enamored. I'm British, after all. American women love the accent." But his heart was speaking up, and it said volumes.

He ignored it, pulled a piece of paper from the drawer of the desk, and began making a list of tasks to complete before the day of the dance. Soon his worries faded as he became consumed with ticking off each item one by one. If he crammed enough work into his days between now and the dance, he wouldn't have time to think about what his heart was doing and could concentrate on leaving. After all, that was the goal, wasn't it? To go back to England?

Wallis left the desk and paced to the other side of the room and back. Blast his heart! It was shouting now. "I dare not stay," he said aloud, and swallowed hard. But ... what if he did?

When Jean got home, she entered the funeral parlor and listened for sounds of men working. She heard nothing, so she went upstairs and listened at the landing. Still nothing. "Whew," she whispered.

She went inside and looked around. Oliver must not have worked up here today. No matter. He and Wallis would be soon enough. In the meantime, should she have dinner with Dora and the rest? She couldn't avoid Wallis forever and had to admit she was curious as to what he wanted to talk about. She wished she could read him better. Was he upset about anything? He didn't seem to be, but she could be wrong.

Jean tried to come up with what it might be but couldn't think of a thing. With a sigh, she went into her bedroom and sat. She should go through her mother's things. She'd need a decent petticoat to go with her new dress.

She left the bedroom and went into the kitchen. The dress still hung by the door. It was beautiful, and she wanted to try it on again, but it would have to wait. If she knew Dora, dinner wasn't far off. She was about to look for the petticoat when she remembered she needed shoes as well. What to do? She couldn't afford new ones, but didn't want to wear what she had. Maybe she could borrow some from Dora?

Jean took a deep breath and left. She'd help Dora with dinner, then ask about the shoes. If Wallis wanted to talk, then so be it. Whatever he had on his mind shouldn't take long to say. She hoped.

When she got to the hotel, Dora was in the kitchen, pouring pan drippings over some roasted chickens. "That smells good. Looks good too."

"Thanks. Phileas and his brothers do like their roast chicken." She spooned more drippings over the birds, then put the pans back in the oven. "Care to help me with the mashed potatoes?"

"Sure." Jean noticed a pot on the stove and got to work. "Where's the butter?"

"In the larder." Dora wiped her hands on her apron and smiled. "So, are you getting excited for the dance?"

Jean sighed. "I need a petticoat. I think my mother had one, but I don't know if Pa gave it away or not."

"In case he did, I have one you can use." She smiled as she went to the icebox. "How's Wallis? I haven't seen him all day."

"He worked on my place, mowed the grass for the dance, then returned Sally and the mower to Mr. Smythe."

Dora brought some milk to the worktable. "Good, it needed to be done."

Jean nodded but said nothing. Part of her was nervous about speaking with him. The other couldn't wait. What if Wallis had something exciting to tell her? Maybe he was sweet on her and wanted to tell her how he felt.

Dora stopped what she was doing. "Are you all right? You look worried."

"Me, no. Just thinking." Jean sat at the table.

Dora knew better. "It's about Wallis, isn't it?"

Jean blushed. "I ... well, I guess it is."

Dora nodded. "It's normal to be nervous when you feel something for someone. Just remember it's also normal to feel scared, but don't let it stop you from being happy."

Jean felt her cheeks flush. Good grief, was it that obvious? "I'm not sure what you mean." Not that playing dumb was going to work on the likes of Dora.

Dora smiled and put her hand on Jean's shoulder. "All I mean is, don't be afraid to tell Wallis how you feel about him. He's a good man and won't think any less of you for being honest about your feelings for him. My pa always said that kind of courage comes with age and experience. But life doesn't always work out the way we plan, so it's important to be brave enough to take risks and speak your mind." She gave Jean a hug and went back to the icebox.

Jean nodded, slightly more at ease. "Please say nothing about this. I was going to talk to him after the dance."

"Suit yourself," Dora said. "But remember, he'll respect your honesty."

Jean nodded. That was fine and dandy, but it was the pain she was afraid of. What if it never went away? Would she live out her days with Wallis permeating her every thought, acute longing her only companion? It was too terrible to think about.

Dora came to the table. "I'm sorry, I didn't mean to upset you."

Jean sighed. "I didn't think it was so obvious. But I have feelings for him. Strong ones, I'm afraid." She studied Dora. Was she falling for Phileas? After all, it's what Wallis was afraid of. Should she ask her?

Dora nodded. "So much has changed since they came here. And it's only been a few weeks."

"I'm not sure it's been that long. Sometimes it feels like the Darlings have been here forever."

Dora smiled. "I'd better get back to work." She left the table and returned to the stove.

Jean watched her a moment, then went the hutch to get the potato masher. She added some milk and butter to the bowl of potatoes, then got to work. As soon as she was done, she put the bowl in the warming oven. What she wouldn't give for a decent-sized cookstove. "I'm going to need a few things from Alma's for my cake. I can use your kitchen, right?"

"Of course." Dora smiled at her. "Sarah told me she spoke to you about the bakery and her house."

"House?"

"Renting it."

Jean nodded. "When I have the money, it could work for me. But I can't think about that right now." For one, she had Wallis to contend with. Maybe a nice hot meal would bolster her courage.

The men filed into the kitchen, checking on dinner. Jean went to set the table, got what she needed from the hutch and took everything into the dining room. If she waited until after the dance to speak to Wallis, she could at least make some nice memories for herself. Then she'd have something to keep her company on lonely nights. She just hoped those memories didn't make things worse.

It wasn't long before Wallis came downstairs. She tried not to look at him, but it was hard. He shaved; his hair combed. He was no longer in his work clothes, but had put on a nice white shirt, gold jacquard vest, green jacket and dark trousers. "Good evening, Jean."

She smiled but said nothing. Seeing him gussied up made her wish she'd changed too. If he looked this good now, what was he going to look like at the dance? Her belly did a flip, and she turned away.

On her way back to the kitchen, she knew she had to wait until after the dance to speak with him. Let the night be something special for them. And who knows? Maybe after spending a nice evening together, Wallis would think about staying.

Jean tried to convince herself of that all the way into the kitchen. By the time she brought the mashed potatoes to the table, she had herself worked up into thinking Wallis would fall in love with her and would stay no matter what. It was a stupid thing to do. Still, at least she decided to speak to him after the dance. Maybe by then she could muster up the courage to say goodbye. Because that's what it was going to come down to. If she was to think of anything, it should be that.

As usual, Wallis sat across the table from her. Jean tried not to look at him, but it was hard. She caught him watching her a few times, and when she did, her belly fluttered and her heart skipped. He was thinking of something, she could tell. Could it be whatever it was he wanted to talk about? Would he pull her aside after dinner? And why couldn't she drop this and think about something else?

She noticed Dora also watched her. Did her friend think she was being foolish? If Dora had figured out she was sweet on Wallis, how many others had? Did Cassie?

What about Sarah? And thank goodness Agnes hadn't. She was too busy looking for any sort of impropriety to notice two people falling in love. Okay, make that one.

Jean's heart ached more than ever, and it was all she could do to make it through the rest of the meal. Now all she had to do was get to the end of the evening without bursting into tears. Unrequited love was the worst kind, and she had to go and find it.

Chapter Seventeen

Wallis watched Jean throughout dinner. She was nervous, and he tried to understand why. Had he said something earlier to upset her? Or was it because Agnes interrupted them in the library? That woman would make anyone nervous with her nagging. He still didn't know how Mr. Featherstone put up with it.

The meal over, he went around the table to Jean and offered a smile. "Did you enjoy the chicken?"

She blushed head to toe. "I did. Thank you."

He eyed her a moment. "You seem nervous about something. Are you?"

She sighed and sat back in her chair. "You wanted to talk to me about something?"

He went stock still. Why was this so hard? It wasn't as if he didn't want to speak to her, but the timing wasn't good. If he spoke to her now, he might ruin the dance for her, not to mention him too. "I ... wonder if you'd like to take a stroll with me?"

She blushed. "You want to go for a walk?"

He smiled and nodded.

She gulped. "Um, okay." She left her chair and headed for the lobby.

He followed and wondered what to say once they got outside. When they left the hotel, he cleared his throat. "I'm, er, glad you joined us for dinner."

"My pleasure."

She didn't look at him – did she not want to be there? "Are you looking forward to the dance?"

"Who isn't?" She clasped her hands behind her back and walked slowly beside him. After a few moments, she gave him a sidelong glance. "Are you going to wear that?"

He glanced at his attire. "No. I have other clothes I brought." He smiled at her. "Ones befitting a dance." His eyes darted to her lips, and he swallowed. Now was not the time to think of kissing her. In fact, it was down-right insane. He wanted to go home, not stay in Apple Blossom. He tried not to look at her, but it was hard.

"Is something wrong?" she asked.

Wallis ran his hand through his hair. He'd forgotten his hat. "Nothing at all." He remembered holding her on the way to the Smythes' place. It made his arms ache to hold her now. Blast it, this wasn't going the way he'd planned. "I'm fine," he finally said. He didn't want her to worry, but eventually she was going to guess that he had feelings for her. The problem was how to hide them.

"Wallis, are you sure?"

He looked at her. "How's the dress?"

Her face screwed up. "What?"

"I ... can't wait to see you in it."

She sighed. "To tell you the truth, I can't wait for you to see me in it either." She smiled shyly. "It's such a lovely color."

He smiled. "I've always loved purple." His eyes gravitated to her mouth again. Blast it. They reached the library, and he thought of sitting on the bench, but didn't dare. His arm would slip around her, then he'd really be in trouble. His resolve to tell her he didn't have any feelings for her was slipping. If this kept up, he'd be proposing instead of ... his eyes went wide. "Oh, dear."

"What?"

He glanced at her, took in her wide eyes, and sucked in a breath. Maybe he had more feelings for her than he thought. Had he been confusing his feelings for Jean with his own resolve to leave? Did that make sense? He wasn't sure. He only knew he wanted to kiss her.

"Wallis?"

He made the mistake of looking into her eyes. "Yes?" By Heaven, she had to be the most beautiful thing he'd ever seen. She looked at him, her lips parting. Before he knew it, he was lowering his head while closing the distance between them. One arm went around her waist as his lips brushed against hers. The kiss was sweet, gentle, and the worst thing he could do. What a dolt!

He broke the kiss, took one look at Jean and gulped.

"That never should have happened. My apologies, I ... don't know what came over me."

She stepped back, her hand to her chest. "I see. Well, you'd best make sure it never happens again." Jean turned on her heel and hurried across the street to the funeral parlor.

Wallis stood like a flummoxed steer. He should go after her but part of him said that would only make things worse. He never should have kissed her in the first place.

He ran his hand through his hair again. "Oh, bother, what have I done?" He headed back to the hotel, his heart beating like a drum. What an idiot. Worse, had anyone seen them? He didn't think so, but one never knew. When he thought about it, the only one that would put up a fuss would be Agnes. She'd take a simple kiss and turn it into who knows what.

He entered the hotel, went upstairs, and once inside his room, sat on the bed. It wasn't long before someone knocked. He rolled his eyes. "Come in."

Oliver opened the door and poked his head in. "Am I bothering you?"

"No, come in."

His brother joined him on the bed. "You looked upset when you came back. Are you all right?"

"No."

"What's wrong?"

Wallis looked at him. "I kissed Jean."

Oliver gasped. "You didn't."

"I'm afraid I did." He flopped backward onto the bed. "That poor girl."

Oliver leaned back on his hands. "So what are you going to do about it?"

"Nothing. I ... made a mistake, that's all."

Oliver laughed. "Wallis, one does not make that sort of mistake without some thought behind it. You had to have *wanted* to kiss her."

"Of course I did. Jean is very attractive. Sweet, kind, the sort one could ..." he stopped himself. "Doesn't matter, we're leaving. I can't get involved with anyone."

"Something tells me you already are."

Wallis sighed and threw his arm over his face. "She's going to hate me."

"Because you're going to leave? If she's in love with you, then yes."

He sat up. "You don't think she is, do you?"

Oliver shrugged. "How should I know?"

He let himself flop against the mattress again. "How did I get into this?"

"How does anyone?" Oliver left the bed. "Are you in love with her?"

Wallis raised his head to look at him. "A good question. What does one feel when they're in love?"

"I'm not the one to ask."

He shut his eyes tight. What a fool he was. Yes, he apologized for the kiss, and told Jean it was a mistake. But how did that make her feel? If she indeed had feelings for him, had he just broken her heart? He sat up again, rubbed his face and sighed. "I'll have to speak with her."

"That would be wise." Oliver got up and headed for the door. "I'm going to my room. You'll figure it out, brother." He faced him. "But if you are in love, do something about it. Don't try to talk yourself into thinking you have to go back to England if you don't want to. Jean deserves better than to have to put up with our mother."

Wallis shuddered. "Let's not bring her up." He also didn't want to have to think too hard about what Oliver had just said. He was implying he'd stay if he was in love with Jean. Was he? He didn't know.

Jean sat on her bed and stared at the wall. She was still in shock that Wallis kissed her. It came out of the blue, and her heart was reeling from it. Then he apologized – he obviously didn't mean to kiss her. Maybe he was curious and wanted to see what kissing her would be like.

Did she like it? In a word, yes. It was magical and took her some place she'd never been before. But now what? If he didn't mean to kiss her, maybe he did it on impulse and nothing more.

She wiped her mouth and looked at her dress. She would enjoy wearing it to the dance. But would she have a good time with Wallis there? Would she be watching him the whole time? Her belly was still fluttering, her mind at a standstill. How could one little kiss do all that?

Jean stood, went to the dress, and took it off the hanger. She brought it to the bed, changed into it, then studied her reflection in her small mirror, adjusting the dress and turning to get a better look. She would indeed enjoy wearing it to the dance. Jean studied her hair next, pulled the pins, then re-plied it on top of her head, trying a different hairstyle.

But it was no use - she still remembered Wallis and his kiss. She wiped her mouth again, as if that would erase the memory, and turned away from the mirror.

She was both excited and apprehensive about going to the dance and didn't know what to do with herself until then. Would Wallis work on her place tomorrow? Could she stand seeing him? But why was she so nervous? Was she expecting something more to happen between them? Or was she worried he'd ignore her the next time they saw each other?

Jean sighed and shook her head. All these questions were making it hard for her to focus on what really mattered: having a good time at the dance. She knew that if she let Wallis distract her too much, it would ruin everything. Taking a deep breath, she closed her eyes and vowed to make the night of the dance one neither of them would ever forget.

She took off the dress, hung it back up and got ready for bed. Tomorrow she'd get what she needed for her cake, then see if she could help with the decorations. If she kept busy enough, she wouldn't have time to think of

Wallis' kiss, or him for that matter. At least she hoped not.

The next morning, she went through her usual morning routine, then left her place and headed to Alma's. When she entered the store, she went straight to the counter and set down her list. Alma, who was doing something in the back of the store, smiled and waved at her. "Good morning. What can I do for you?"

Jean smiled and headed her way. "I need some ingredients for a chocolate cake. I'm making it for the dance."

"Ohhh, chocolate is expensive, but I have some." Alma went behind the counter and pulled a tin box off a shelf. She set it on the counter and opened it. "How much do you need?"

Jean showed her the recipe. "I'll need more sugar too."

"Anything else?"

"Let me look at some ribbon." She went to the table covered with various fripperies: hair ribbons, combs, hat pins, brushes, and skeins of lace. She picked up some purple ribbon that matched her dress. "This is pretty."

"It is, isn't it?" Alma joined her at the table. "You could wear either the purple or the white. Both would match."

"The white, I think." Jean picked up the spool of ribbon and handed it to Alma. Would Wallis like it? She sighed. She had to stop thinking about him.

Alma took the ribbon to the counter. "Do you need anything else?"

"No, that's it for now." But Jean continued to look around the store. There were lots of things she'd like but couldn't afford. That Wallis bought her a dress was a reminder of that.

She stared at the floor. In a few days, she would go to the dance, have the best time of her life, then have to say goodbye to Wallis Darling. Their parting was inevitable. He'd given no signs he wanted to stay. There was nothing to keep him here. And when he was gone, she'd just have to move on.

Alma gathered the rest of what she needed and rang it up. "The decorating committee is coming here at noon, if you'd care to help."

"Thanks. I think I will." Jean left the store and went down the street to her place. She looked at the dismal exterior and tried to picture it yellow with white trim. Fresh paint would brighten the place up and give it a cheerful appearance. It surprised her she hadn't seen Wallis or Oliver yet. They already had the paint.

She went inside and headed upstairs. After putting everything away, she decided to fetch the shoes she was going to borrow from Dora. When she went down again, Wallis was there. "Oh, hello." She blushed something fierce.

So did he. "Hi." He went to the storeroom and stepped inside. When he came out, he had a can of paint in each hand.

"So you're painting today," she said.

He nodded, and she noticed he wasn't making eye contact.

"Where's Oliver?"

"He'll be along." Wallis headed for the door. "I'm going to take this out back and get things ready."

Like an idiot, she followed. "Can I help?"

He was outside now and turned to look at her. One would think she'd just asked him to burn down the building. "Um, if you'd like."

Jean forced a smile. She shouldn't be doing this. Spending more time with him was only going to lead to trouble. But she couldn't help herself. She was so drawn to him, and she couldn't explain why. Well, other than the obvious. Drat love, anyway. "On second thought," she said. "Alma told me that the decorating committee was meeting in the store later. I should be there."

"Very well. Oliver and I can handle this well enough." He pried the lid off a can of paint.

Jean turned to leave.

"I do apologize for last night."

She froze. "There's no need to do it again."

She didn't turn around but heard him approach. "I am sorry, Jean."

She swallowed hard and closed her eyes. "So am I." She started walking. That was as close as she was going to get to telling him how she felt.

Without another word, Jean went down the street and marched back into Alma's store.

§&

Wallis watched Jean go, his heart in his throat. He saw the hurt in her eyes, and wanted to do something about it, but what? Worse, he was the one that put it there.

When Oliver arrived, he had the paint mixed and ready. He handed Oliver a brush, and they got to work. It wasn't long before they needed a ladder and went to the livery stable to borrow one from Etta. "We hate to ask," Wallis said. "But we won't need it long."

Etta, a petite, dark-haired young woman with big blue eyes, smiled at them. "Go ahead. I'm not using it right now." She patted the neck of the horse she was shoeing. "Just keep it until you're done."

Oliver smiled, tipped his hat, then headed for the ladder leaning against one wall.

"What color are you painting Jean's place?"

Oliver answered before Wallis could. "Yellow, with white trim. Think of how cheery it will look."

Etta walked around the horse with a laugh. "It's a funeral parlor. It's not supposed to be cheery."

"All the more reason to make it that way," Wallis said. "Don't you think this town has had enough gloom hanging over it?"

Etta shrugged. "If you put it the way." She went around the horse and got back to work.

Wallis watched her a moment before he and Oliver carried the ladder down the street and behind the building. He'd noticed the residents of Apple Blossom didn't talk about the incident any more than they had to.

They got to work and were soon painting the upper half of the building. At the rate they were going, they'd have the building and most of the trim done by the night of the dance. He liked the work and that it helped keep his mind off things.

The day wore on, and when they went to work on the front of the building, he spied Jean on the porch of the general store, talking with Alma. When she was done, she glanced his way, then headed for the hotel. Okay, fine, she didn't want to talk to him. He couldn't blame her. If he were smart, he wouldn't have said anything to her in the first place. But it was too late for that now. So what was he going to do? Should he leave her alone until the dance? Try to speak to her again? If he apologized a third time, would that make things worse and hurt her more?

"Let her be," Oliver suggested.

Wallis turned to him. "How do you know what I was thinking?"

His brother smiled. "Because you have the same look on your face you always get when you're making a big decision."

"It's not that big."

"Isn't it?"

Wallis dipped his brush in the paint. "I made one little mistake. There's no need to make a fuss over it."

Oliver sighed. "Are you sure your heart isn't?"

Drat, he had him there. "So what if it is?"

"Then hadn't you better do something about it?" Oliver looked over what they'd just painted. "We're about done here. Time to tackle the upper half."

Wallis watched him head for the ladder. He followed, for lack of a better idea, and got back to work. He'd give Jean her space for now and speak to her at the dance. Then he'd apologize again if he must and take things from there. It was all he could do at this point. After the dance, he'd speak with Sterling about the parsonage. Sterling, Conrad and Irving could work on it. The rest of them were going home. In fact, he'd talk to his brothers about a set return date. That way they had a deadline. Not that they didn't already, but he wanted to move it up.

Maybe then he wouldn't be hesitant when the time came to leave. Because at this point, if his heart had its way, it would have him stay.

Chapter Eighteen

By the time the dance rolled around, Jean had hardly seen Wallis. She kept busy with the library, gathering more donations, and cataloguing all the new books. She'd taken in quite a few by going to the local farms and ranches to tell people about the library and let them know it was now open.

Everyone she talked to was interested and several came to town yesterday to check out books. Reading was one of the principal forms of entertainment in Apple Blossom, and with the dance, folks that normally wouldn't come other than to attend church or get supplies had something extra to take part in.

The decoration committee made flower garlands for the food tables, and some women loaned their nice tablecloths for the occasion. Everyone talked about their dresses and how excited they were. This was the biggest thing to happen in Apple Blossom in a long time and no one wanted to waste the evening.

Jean had Dora help her with her hair, and the transformation a new hairstyle could give amazed her. Dora wove the white ribbon she purchased through loops of hair and the look was stunning. She could hardly recognize herself. Now here she was, standing next to a refreshment table, waiting for Wallis and the rest of his brothers to show up. Why they were running late, she didn't know.

But it figured. She knew she and Wallis would talk tonight. Should she start the conversation, or let him do it? Maybe when he spotted her, he'd want to speak right away. Would it ruin her evening if he told her he wanted nothing to do with her romantically? She shut her eyes against the thought. Despite the risk of a broken heart, she still wanted the evening to be magical.

She wiped away a stray tear. This was the best she'd ever looked and wished Pa could see her like this.

Laughter carried across the dance area and her head came up. She didn't realize she'd been staring at the ground. She wiped her eyes again, then spied Wallis on the other side of the dance floor. Captain Stanley still hadn't returned from Bozeman, and so there were only a few musicians. Mrs. Smythe could play the piano and Mr. Atkins had a fiddle. Mr. Watson also offered to play his guitar.

Oliver was suddenly at her side. "Good evening, Jean. May I say you look lovely this evening."

"You may." Jean hoped her eyes weren't red. She'd done her share of crying over the last couple of days. She figured if she got it out of her system before the dance, there would be less chance of her weeping when she got around to talking to Wallis. She wasn't sure about that now.

Jean saw Wallis cut through the crowd, heading right for her. He didn't want to talk now, did he?

"Something wrong?" Oliver asked. "You look pale."

Jean shook her head. Wallis was getting closer. "I'm fine."

Oliver saw Wallis and waved at him. "I think my brother is hoping for the first dance."

Jean took a deep breath, bracing herself. "That's fine."

He turned to her. "Are you sure about that?"

She glanced at him. "Is there something you know I don't?"

Oliver shook his head. "Just asking."

She nodded and waited for Wallis to approach. When he reached her, he grinned. "Good evening, Jean." His eyes roamed over her. "You look lovely this evening." He swallowed hard. "Enchanting." His eyes met hers. "May I have the honor of the first dance?"

Jean stared at him, her heart in her throat. Goodness gracious, she couldn't even talk! How did he do this to her? She moved her mouth a few times but still nothing came out. She settled for a nod.

Wallis smiled as the piano played, soon joined by Mr.

Atkins' fiddle. People slowly but surely went to the dance area, and the dancing started.

"Shall we?" Wallis said and offered his arm.

She stared at it a moment, then looped her arm through his. He led her toward several couples already dancing, including Sterling and Letty. They looked to be having a wonderful time. Too bad she wasn't. Her heart was in her throat as Wallis turned to her and took her hands in his. It was a simple country dance, and it didn't surprise her that he knew it.

Wallis looked into her eyes as they danced, their blue depths drawing her in as they never had before. She was becoming lost in them and could gaze at him all night. But that wasn't about to happen. Yet why was he looking at her like this? Was it because he was leaving soon? Yes, that must be it. Maybe he was trying to memorize her face at the same time she was trying to memorize his.

Her heart pounded at the thought and her mouth went dry. At this rate, she wasn't sure she could make it through the evening. The music was festive, but for her, it might well be a funeral dirge. This was the last time she would see him like this. Soon he would be gone and then what? Even though her friends would still be here, she would have a hole in her heart the size of Montana. One far bigger than the one she had before the Darlings showed up.

"You're being quiet," he commented.

She looked at him. "I know. I ... have lot on my mind."

He brought his face closer to hers. "Like what, Jean?"

She swallowed hard. It was now or never. "Well, if you must know, you."

He said nothing at first. Instead, he looked into her eyes and sighed. "Have you been thinking of me often these last few days?"

Something between a laugh and a sob escaped her. "Perhaps." She would not cry, she would not cry. "Have you been thinking of me?"

His face drew closer. "I have."

She swallowed hard. He wasn't going to kiss her again, was he? Not in front of all these people. More had come onto the grassy dance floor, and the noise of their chatter would make listening to Wallis difficult. "Did you have anything you wanted to say to me?" she asked.

He looked into her eyes again. "I do."

She shut her eyes tight a moment. "Go ahead, get it out."

When she opened them, he was looking around. "Here, now?"

She nodded. "Why not?"

Wallis drew closer, his eyes fixed on hers. "Jean, I don't know how to say this."

She sniffed tears that weren't there. Yet. "Then I'll say it for you."

His eyebrows shot up. "How do you know what I want to say?"

"Because I've been thinking about it for days. I know what I'd want to say to me if I were you."

One eyebrow arched. "Do you, now?"

She nodded. "You're leaving, Wallis. We both know it. And there's no use trying to ignore the fact any longer. So one of us might as well say it."

He stared at her as his other eyebrow went up. One side of his mouth looked like it was curving into a smile. But the light was low, so how could she be sure? "Then tell me, Jean. Tell me goodbye."

Her breathing picked up, and the words left her. She'd even rehearsed them in front of her mirror a few times, while Wallis and Oliver had been outside painting the building. She couldn't do it then and found she couldn't do it now. Her jaw trembled. "Oh, Wallis ..." She tried to pull away.

But he held her fast. "Jean." He pulled her closer than he ought to. Had the music stopped? She didn't know. All she knew was that he was holding her as close as he did when he kissed her. "I've been thinking a lot about what I wanted to say to you, and I'm sorry to say that 'goodbye' wasn't part of it."

Her eyes went wide. "What?"

He pulled her closer still. "The truth is, I love you."

Her knees buckled.

"What did you just say?" someone snapped.

In the back of Jean's mind, she knew who it was. Agnes.

Sure enough, Agnes pushed her way through the townsfolk until she stood beside them. "Unhand her this instant!"

Wallis frowned. "Oh, bugger off."

Agnes gasped. "*What* did you just say?"

"Go away." Wallis pulled Jean against him. "Can't you see I'm trying to convey to the lady my deepest feelings?"

Agnes gasped again. "No! Not another one of you! I won't have it!" She took Jean by the arm and tried to pull her away from him.

Wallis wasn't having it. "My good woman, if you don't take your hands off Jean, I will escort you to your husband and inform him of your interference in my affairs."

"Oh, stuff and nonsense," Agnes whined. "Now get out of here. Can't you see you're upsetting Jean?"

Wallis looked at her. "Darling, you're crying."

Jean nodded. She was still trying to figure out if she'd heard him right. "What did you say to me?"

He took her by the arms. "I love you. I can't fight it anymore. I won't. This thing between us has been driving me insane these last few days." He pulled her closer. "Jean, I don't know what the future for us will hold, but I know this. I love you. I think I have for a while now. To avoid it, I turned to my sense of duty."

"To return to England, you mean?"

"Yes."

Agnes groaned and pinched the bridge of her nose.

This time Jean looked at her. "Really, Agnes. Go get yourself some punch or something."

Agnes glared at them. "You're making a spectacle of yourself, Jean Campbell. This is a public outrage!"

"No," Wallis said with a grin. "This is love." He got down on one knee.

Jean thought she might faint. "Wallis?"

He looked into her eyes and smiled. "Jean, I know it hasn't been long. But in the few weeks I've known you, I've grown to love you. Therefore I'm proud to make, as Agnes calls it, a public spectacle of myself." He took her hands in his. "Jean Campbell, I love you. I don't know if you feel the same about me. In the hope that you do, I ask for your hand in marriage."

She stood stock still. Was this really happening? Did she need to pinch herself? She glanced at Agnes, who glared back, then looked around. The music had stopped, and everyone present had formed a circle around them. Every eye was fixed on her, waiting for her answer. She looked at Wallis, her heart in her throat. This wasn't what she expected. Goodbyes, yes; a proposal, no.

"I'm sorry if this has come as a shock ..."

Jean shook her head. "No ... I ..." She saw the smiling faces around them. The only one frowning was Agnes. Finally, Jean smiled too. "I love you, Wallis. That's what I wanted to talk to you about the other day."

He grinned. "Then give me your answer, Jean. Will you marry me?"

She smiled back, tears in her eyes. "Yes!"

He jumped to his feet and pulled her into his arms. "Oh, my darling, you've made me so happy."

Sterling was there, staring at Agnes, who slinked into the cheering townspeople and disappeared. As soon as she was gone, he smiled at them. "Well, well. Congratulations, you two. I had a feeling."

"Only because I told you," Oliver quipped.

"There was that." Sterling smiled again. "Will love never take its hand off this place?"

Oliver blanched and looked at Phileas, who looked at the nearest people around him. Dora was nowhere in sight and Jean wondered if her friend might be next. But right now, she didn't care. Wallis had proposed! But ... now what? The town had no preacher. Who knew when they'd be able to get married? Would he return to England anyway?

"Darling," he whispered. "You look worried." He glanced around, took her arm and steered her away from the crowd. People slapped them on the backs and gave words of congratulations as they passed. By the time they reached the edge of the dance area, Jean didn't know if she was coming or going. Wallis pulled her past the refreshment tables and into the shadows.

"What are we doing way over here?" she asked.

"Oh, let everyone think I'm stealing a kiss. I did just ask you to marry me."

She smiled at him in the dim light. "Yes, I still can't believe it."

He pulled her into his arms. "Believe it." He lowered his face to hers and kissed her.

Jean melted against him. This was not the chaste kiss

he'd given her a few days ago. This kiss was so much more. Her heart stopped for a moment as all thought left. There was only him, and even the sound of the dance faded away.

When Wallis broke the kiss, he looked into her eyes and smiled. "I'm such a fool. Can you forgive me?"

"Fool?"

"For not listening to my heart and figuring out what was happening sooner. You stirred a passion within me, Jean. I mistook it for my zeal for duty. I'm afraid I've never been in love before, so it took me a while to sort things out."

She smiled. "You're forgiven."

His smile faded before he glanced at the festivities. "Can you forgive me for something else?"

She searched his face, his eyes. He looked concerned. "What is it?"

"Well, we haven't been completely honest with you."

"We?"

"My brothers and me. You see, our name isn't Darling, but Darlington. We're traveling under the other name to avoid trouble. We didn't want to draw attention to ourselves during our travels."

She shook her head in confusion. "I don't understand. Why would you?"

Wallis looked her in the eyes. "Our father is the Viscount Darlington of Sussex. Sterling, as the eldest, will inherit. That is, if he'll take it. He can't very well run a vast estate from here, can he?"

Jean gaped at him a moment. "Pardon my ignorance, but ... what's a viscount?"

He shrugged. "Well, as far as the order of nobility goes, there's a duke, then a marquess. After that comes an earl, then a viscount and after that, a baron."

She stared at him in confusion. She knew nothing of this sort of thing. "Then where do knights fit in?"

"Below the barons."

She swallowed hard. "So ... so you and your brothers come from nobility?"

He nodded.

"But ... I thought you were landowners. Farmers."

"Indeed, we are. Our tenants are our farmers, though we help."

"Tenants?"

"Those that work our land. We have about twenty tenants at present and a considerably large estate."

Her jaw dropped. "You mean ... you're rich?"

"Well, not extravagantly wealthy, but we are well off."

She stared into the darkness as everything sank in. "So that's why you want to make sure Phileas returns to England. He'd be the one to take things over for your father if your other brothers don't go back."

"Yes, and now the pressure on poor Phileas to do so has increased tenfold. I don't know what my brother will do at this point. He has yet to sink his teeth into the hotel. But enough of all that." He pulled her close again, bent his head to hers and kissed her soundly.

Jean let go of everything he told her and let his kiss

take her where it would. This one was gentle, slow, and full of promise. She couldn't wait to see what that promise would entail. Her life was forever changed from this moment on, and the horrible hole left behind by her father's death filled to the brim with Wallis' profession of love and proposal. In a few moments he'd made her the happiest woman in town! Maybe the entire territory. There was so much to do and plan now. She prayed Captain Stanley found a preacher. Why else would he not be back yet?

When Wallis broke the kiss he hugged her, then offered his arm. "We should get back."

She blushed head to toe. "What if I don't want to?"

"And give Agnes more ammunition to accuse us of who knows what?"

She sighed. "You're right. That could be a big what. That is, she'd try to make it into one."

"Indeed." He smiled at her. "Do you forgive my brothers and me?"

Jean put her hand to his cheek. "Of course, I do. You were protecting yourselves." She glanced at the dance. "Do the others know?"

"If you're referring to Letty, Cassie, and Sarah, yes. They know."

She took a breath, let it out slowly. "Okay, then I suspect you want me to keep this a secret?"

"I would appreciate it." He kissed her on the cheek.

"I'll be silent as the grave."

He laughed. "Thank you."

"What's so funny?"

"Well, you are the undertaker."

She laughed. "So I am."

He kissed her again and escorted her back to the others. To Wallis it didn't matter if she was an undertaker, a baker, or a blacksmith. He fell in love with her just as she was.

Jean smiled at the thought as he steered her onto the grassy dance floor, bowed, then took her into his arms and began to dance.

THE END

About the Author

Kit Morgan has written for fun all her life. Whether she's writing contemporary or historical romance, her whimsical stories are fun, inspirational, sweet and clean, and depict a strong sense of family and community. Raised by a homicide detective, one would think she'd write suspense, (and yes, she plans to get around to those eventually, cozy mysteries too!) but Kit likes fun and romantic westerns! Kit resides in the beautiful Pacific Northwest in a little log cabin on Clear Creek, after which her fictional town that appears in many of her books is named.

Want to get in on the fun?

Find out about new releases, cover reveals, bonus content, fun times and more? Join Kit's Newsletter at www.authorkitmorgan.com

Printed in Great Britain
by Amazon